"You want me."

"All right!" yelled Phoebe. "I do want you. Saturday night was amazing. I do want a repeat. But it's not going to happen."

Alex shoved his hands through his hair. "Why the hell not?"

She gaped. "You make me lose control. You distort my focus. My judgment derails when I get distracted and I can't risk that. I won't compromise that for a brief fling with you. It's just not worth it."

LUCY KING spent her formative years lost in the world of Harlequin romance when she really ought to have been paying attention to her teachers. Up against sparkling heroines, gorgeous heroes and the magic of falling in love, trigonometry and absolute ablatives didn't stand a chance.

But as she couldn't live in a dream world forever, she eventually acquired a degree in languages and an eclectic collection of jobs. A stroll to the River Thames one Saturday morning led her to her very own hero. The minute she laid eyes on the hunky rower getting out of a boat, clad only in Lycra and carrying a three-meter oar as if it was a toothpick, she knew she'd met the man she was going to marry. Luckily the rower thought the same.

She will always be grateful to whatever it was that made her stop dithering and actually sit down to type Chapter One, because dreaming up her own sparkling heroines and gorgeous heroes is pretty much her idea of the perfect job.

Originally a Londoner, Lucy now lives in Spain, where she spends much of the time reading, failing to finish cryptic crosswords and trying to convince herself that lying on the beach really is the best way to work. Visit her at www.lucyking.net.

PROPOSITIONED BY THE BILLIONAIRE

LUCY KING

~ Jet Set Billionaires ~

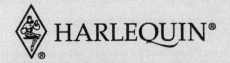

HARLEQUIN®

TORONTO • NEW YORK • LONDON
AMSTERDAM • PARIS • SYDNEY • HAMBURG
STOCKHOLM • ATHENS • TOKYO • MILAN • MADRID
PRAGUE • WARSAW • BUDAPEST • AUCKLAND

If you purchased this book without a cover you should be aware
that this book is stolen property. It was reported as "unsold and
destroyed" to the publisher, and neither the author nor the
publisher has received any payment for this "stripped book."

Recycling programs
for this product may
not exist in your area.

ISBN-13: 978-0-373-52784-7

PROPOSITIONED BY THE BILLIONAIRE

First North American Publication 2010.

Copyright © 2010 by Lucy King.

All rights reserved. Except for use in any review, the reproduction or
utilization of this work in whole or in part in any form by any electronic,
mechanical or other means, now known or hereafter invented, including
xerography, photocopying and recording, or in any information storage
or retrieval system, is forbidden without the written permission of the
publisher, Harlequin Enterprises Limited, 225 Duncan Mill Road,
Don Mills, Ontario, Canada M3B 3K9.

This is a work of fiction. Names, characters, places and incidents are
either the product of the author's imagination or are used fictitiously,
and any resemblance to actual persons, living or dead, business
establishments, events or locales is entirely coincidental.

This edition published by arrangement with Harlequin Books S.A.

For questions and comments about the quality of this book
please contact us at Customer_eCare@Harlequin.ca.

® and ™ are trademarks of the publisher. Trademarks indicated with
® are registered in the United States Patent and Trademark Office, the
Canadian Trade Marks Office and in other countries.

www.eHarlequin.com

Printed in U.S.A.

PROPOSITIONED BY
THE BILLIONAIRE

For Justin—possibly the most patient man
on the planet

CHAPTER ONE

'MARK, STEP AWAY from the flamingo and get out of the pond. Please.'

Phoebe heard the note of desperation in her voice and prayed it would be enough to penetrate the alcohol-fogged brain of the man who was lurching around the pond and brandishing a bottle of champagne.

'Darling,' slurred Mark as he swung round and threw her a lopsided grin while water lilies slapped around his knees. 'You keep trying to persuade me to get out, but I don't want to.'

He waggled his finger at her and her spirits sank. No amount of cajoling or threatening had had the slightest effect so why on earth had she thought desperation would have worked?

'That much is obvious,' she muttered and racked her brains for a solution. Dealing with problems was part of her job, but right now she was stumped.

'I have a suggestion.' He swayed wildly and Phoebe's heart skipped a beat.

Unless he revealed that he planned to take himself off somewhere quiet and sober up, preferably on the other side of London, she didn't think she wanted to hear it. 'What is it?'

Mark spread his arms wide and grinned. 'Why don't you jump in and join me? The water's great and I'd like to introduce you to my new friend.' He turned and stumbled after the flamingo, which had hopped out of range and was now preening its feathers.

Phoebe shivered and sighed and wondered what she'd done to deserve this. It had clearly been far too much to hope that this evening might remain trouble free, but for a moment everything had been going so well.

So the opulent crimson and silver theme that ran throughout the bar wasn't really to her taste, and the huge chandeliers that sprinkled light over the glittering throng were, in her opinion, totally over the top. And as for allowing birds to wander freely around the gardens six storeys above street level, well, that, as this little episode had proved, was a recipe for disaster, however unique and fashionable.

However, none of that mattered. Not one little bit.

All that mattered was that the San Lorenzo Roof Gardens was the trendiest new venue in town. It was *the* place to hold a pre-launch party for a hip young handbag designer, and it was virtually impossible to book.

But she'd done it. She'd spent weeks flattering the unyielding Mr Bogoni until he'd cracked and agreed to let her hire the venue, and had then poured hours of meticulous planning and endless preparation into ensuring that this would be a party that people would gossip about for months.

Inside the bar buzzed with a subtle air of excitement and expectation, fuelled by exquisite canapés and the finest champagne. Jo's gemstone-encrusted handbags sat high on their individually spotlit pedestals, refracting the light like multicoloured glitter balls, and the star of the show herself was mingling among the one hundred glamorous guests and chatting to the carefully selected journalists as if she'd been doing it for years instead of an hour.

Jo Douglas, Phoebe's first and currently only client, was heading for the stratosphere, and the fledgling Jackson Communications would soar right alongside her.

So she was *not* going to stand back and let Jo's boyfriend ruin an evening she'd worked so hard to put together.

Phoebe's jaw set. There was only one thing for it. She had to get rid of Mark. Discreetly and quickly before someone with a camera decided to step out for a breath of fresh air. And as the bar was getting warmer by the minute, she didn't have any time to lose.

Right. Phoebe broke a twig off an overhanging branch and stuck it between her teeth. She twisted her hair into a thick rope, wound it deftly onto the top of her head and secured it with the twig. Then she slipped out of her shoes and wriggled to hitch her dress up her thighs.

Taking a deep fortifying breath and trying not to think about what might lurk beneath the surface of the water, she gave herself a quick shake, straightened her spine and set her sights on her target.

'Do you need a hand?'

The deep voice came from behind her and Phoebe shrieked, jumped almost a foot into the air and nearly pitched headlong into the pond. She spun round, her hand flying to her throat and her heart thundering as a large shadowy figure leaning against a tree swam into vision. 'Who are you?' she squeaked when she was able to breathe again.

'Someone who thinks you look like you could do with some help.' He pushed himself off the tree and gestured to Mark as he took a step towards her.

Phoebe's hand automatically shot out to stop him coming any closer and then she dropped it, feeling faintly foolish. Wherever he'd sprung from he was hardly likely to be going to attack her. 'If leaping out of nowhere and scaring me witless is your idea of helping, thank you, but no.'

He stopped and tilted his head. 'Sure?'

'Quite sure,' she said, resisting the urge to glance down to check the ground beneath her feet. His lazy drawl was having the oddest effect on her equilibrium. Either that, or London was in the unlikely grip of an earthquake. 'What are you doing out here anyway?'

'Admiring the scenery.'

Somehow she knew he wasn't referring to the landscaping and she felt a kick of something in the pit of her stomach. 'You should be inside admiring the handbags.'

'Not really my thing.'

'Then perhaps you're at the wrong party.' Phoebe frowned. Come to think of it, he hadn't actually answered her question. She'd met and ticked off everyone on the guest list, and none of them had had such an impressive outline. So who the hell was he?

Phoebe ran her gaze over him, momentarily forgetting what was going on behind her, and found herself wondering what he looked like. Part of her longed for him to step into the light so she could get a proper look at him and see if his looks matched up to his voice. The other toyed with the idea of summoning the bouncers.

Because whoever he was, this was a private party and

if he wasn't on the guest list then he was gatecrashing. In fact, she thought, pulling herself together, he could well have sneaked in while she'd been in Mr Bogoni's office, staring at the fuzzy CCTV feed and simultaneously trying to swallow her astonishment, placate the volatile Italian and ignore his mutterings about suing for damages should anything happen to the flamingo.

'I'm at exactly the right party. And it's turned out to be far more interesting than I could possibly have imagined.'

Phoebe frowned and was just about to demand his invitation when she heard a series of splashes behind her. A shower of cool water hit the backs of her legs and she stifled a squeal of shock. Mark must have got bored with the flamingo, thank goodness, and decided to come over and investigate this latest development.

'I suspect the show's nearly over.'

'That's a shame. I was enjoying it.'

Despite the warmth of the night she shivered. 'There's far better entertainment inside. Drinks, music, dancing. Much more exciting.'

'I'm inclined to disagree,' he said softly and her heart thumped. 'Besides, I've spent the past sixteen hours either in a car or on a plane. At this stage of the evening fresh air is a novelty.'

'Plenty of fresh air on the other side of the bar. As you can see, I'm afraid I have things to attend to.'

As soon as Mark stumbled to within reaching distance she'd pull him out and bundle him off herself.

'Do you really think you can handle this on your own?'

If she'd been able to see his face properly she was sure she'd find a patronising smile hovering at his lips and Phoebe bristled. She'd been handling things on her own for years. 'Of course.'

He folded his arms over his chest and shrugged. 'In that case I'll stay out of your way.'

'Thank you,' she said crisply and turned back.

Mark was far closer that she'd thought and was waving the bottle of champagne even more wildly than before. All he had to do was trip and he'd land right on top of her.

It was now or never. Phoebe reached out to grab him but he reeled back, teetering as if balancing on the edge of a precipice and then pitched forward. Flailing around while desperately trying to cling onto his balance, his arm and the hand holding the bottle swung round in her direction. An arc of champagne sprayed through the air. Phoebe let out a little cry and jerked back, her hands flying to her head.

Oh no, not her hair. Please not her hair.

She didn't have time to recover and pull Mark out. A split second later a pair of large hands clamped round her waist and shoved her to one side. She yelped in shock and watched in stunned appal as the shadowy stranger grabbed Mark by the T-shirt and hauled him out of the water.

'Hey, what are you doing?' Mark yelled, splashing frantically as the bottle of champagne landed in the water with a plop.

Good question, thought Phoebe dazedly, her skin beneath her dress burning where his hands had gripped her.

'Taking out the rubbish,' he snarled and leaned in very close. 'Men like you belong behind bars.'

'What are you talking about?' Mark spluttered. 'Get off me. You can't do this. I'll sue.'

'Go right ahead,' he growled.

'You'll be sorry.'

'I doubt it. Wait here,' he snapped at Phoebe, and then dragged Mark, kicking and struggling, across the garden.

Wait here?

For a moment Phoebe had no choice in the matter. She stood frozen to the spot, droplets of icy water clinging to her bare legs, her heart hammering while shock reverberated around her and the outraged sound of Mark's protests and threats rang in her ears.

In dumb stupefaction she watched the two men disappear round the corner and struggled to make sense of what had just gone on. Maybe she'd been hurled into a third-rate action film, because in reality men didn't just leap out of nowhere, elbow their way into the action and then march off leaving chaos trailing in their wake like a brief but devastating tornado. At least, not in her experience.

As her shock receded the potential consequences of this little episode filtered into her head. How dared he barge in like that? When she'd told him in no uncertain terms that she was in control of the situation. Did he have any idea of the damage he could have done?

And then barking at her to wait. What did he expect her to do? Hang around like some sort of obedient minion? Hah, she thought, bending down to pick up her shoes. As if. She had to go and find out whether any journalistic or photographic prying eyes had caught what had just happened and if necessary execute a hasty damage-limitation exercise.

Who did he think he was anyway, creeping up on her like that and scaring the living daylights out of her? And manhandling Mark like some sort of brutish Neanderthal.

Kind of attractive though. That single-mindedness. That decisiveness. That strength…

Phoebe slapped her hand against her forehead. No no no no *no*. That was so wrong on so many levels she didn't know where to start. Focus. That was what she needed. Focus. And her heels.

As she searched for something sturdy to lean against while she put her shoes back on again Phoebe's skin suddenly prickled all over.

Her head shot round and her eyes narrowed in on the man striding in her direction, alone. Tall, broad-shouldered and flexing his hands, he moved in a sort of intensely purposeful way that had her stomach clenching.

In irritation, she decided, straightening and preparing herself for confrontation. Definitely irritation.

As his long strides closed the distance between them she could see that his face was as dark as the suit that moulded to his body. But what he had to glower about she had no idea. If anyone had the right to be furious it was her.

Phoebe's heart began to thud. Forget the shoes. Damage limitation could wait. Adrenalin surged through her. 'You frightened the life out of me,' she said, when he got within hissing distance, her voice low and tight with anger. 'Who are you and what on earth did you think you were doing?'

He didn't reply, merely took her arm and wheeled her off towards the pergola at the bottom of the wide stone steps that led up to the terrace. Phoebe had no option but to stagger after him, shoes dangling from her fingers as panic and shock flooded back into every bone in her body.

'Hang on,' she said, desperately trying to keep her voice down. 'You can't throw me out too. Ow!' The smooth paving stones had turned into sharp gravel, which dug into the soles of her feet.

He stopped, looked down as she hopped madly while trying to put her shoes back on and then, muttering a brief curse under his breath, swept her up into his arms. Phoebe let out a tiny squeal as her shoulder slapped against a rock-hard chest. One of his hands planted itself on the side of her breast, the other wrapped around her bare thigh.

'Put me down!' she whispered furiously, her legs bouncing with every step he took as she tried to tug down her dress in a vain attempt to protect her modesty.

He stopped beneath a lantern and set her on her feet, her body brushing against his in the process. A flurry of tingles whizzed round her and she wobbled. He wound one arm round her waist and clamped her against him.

'I have no intention of throwing you out,' he said roughly, raking his gaze over her face.

'So let me go.'

If anything, his arm tightened and Phoebe felt as if someone had plugged her into a socket. What else could explain the tingles and sparks that zapped through her? What else could account for the searing heat that swept along her veins, making her bones melt and turning her spine to water?

'My name is Alex and you should choose your boyfriends more carefully.'

At the icy restraint lacing his voice, Phoebe's eyes jerked to his and for a moment she forgot how to breathe.

Oh, dear God. His eyes were mesmerising. Grey. No, not just grey. Silver, rapidly darkening to slate, and fringed with the thickest eyelashes she'd ever seen on a man. Set beneath straight dark eyebrows and blazing down at her with fierce concern.

As she dragged her gaze over the planes of his face

in much the same way as he was now doing to her. Phoebe's mouth went dry and the blood in her veins grew hot and sluggish. He wasn't just handsome. He was jaw-droppingly gorgeous. But not in the pretty way the men who occupied her world were. This man looked like the sort of man who knew how to do, and probably did, the things that real men were supposed to do.

The little white scar above his right eye and the hint of a broken nose gave him an air of danger that she might have considered to be intoxicating if she'd been in the market for a man. Which she wasn't. But heavens, that mouth. What a mouth...

Her hands, currently curled into fists and jammed between his chest and hers, itched to unfurl themselves, creep their way up the thick white cotton shirt, maybe taking in a quick detour to the V of tanned flesh exposed where his top button was undone, and up, round his neck to wind themselves in his hair so that they could tug that delicious-looking mouth down and weld it to hers.

Phoebe blinked. Agh. What on earth was she thinking? Her body had no business behaving like this, especially without her prior approval. And that would not be forthcoming this evening. Or ever, she reminded herself belatedly, pushing all thoughts of what sort of things a real man might be required to do out of her head.

Giving herself a mental shake, she forced herself to concentrate. What had he been saying? She thought frantically. Boyfriends. That was it. 'What boyfriend?' she managed, squeezing her hands tighter and hauling back some of the self-control that had fled when he'd pulled her against him.

'The jerk in the pond.'

'He's not my boyfriend.' After her last disastrous relationship, she was off men. For ever. Especially ones who crept up on her and nearly gave her a heart attack. However good-looking.

'Did he hurt you?'

'No. Of course not.' What was he talking about? She struggled to pull herself out of the steel circle of his arm, but it was no good. Alex didn't seem inclined to let her go.

Instead he gripped her chin with his long brown fingers and turned her face so that the light fell on her cheek. 'He took a swing at you with the bottle,' he said harshly. 'Where did he hit you?'

Phoebe's skin sizzled beneath the pressure of his fingers. 'Have you lost your mind?' she said, baffled as much by the tingles shooting through her as the direction of the conversation. 'Mark didn't hit me.'

'Are you sure?'

'Of course I'm sure,' she said. 'I think I might have noticed if I'd been thwacked by a bottle of champagne. Particularly vintage.'

His mouth tightened. 'Not funny.'

'I couldn't agree more,' she said sharply. There was absolutely nothing funny about the damage he could have done tonight, possibly the most important night of her and Jo's lives. 'Can I have my chin back?'

He let her chin go as if it were on fire and she swung her head round to glare up at him. For a moment they simply stared at each other and Phoebe became aware that, still locked in his vice-like embrace as she was, every inch of her body pressed up against every hard-muscled inch of his.

Heat pooled in the pit of her stomach and her heart thumped. Her mouth dried and she swallowed. She *had* to get a grip. And not of his biceps. 'Right. So you barged in because you thought my boyfriend had hit me?' A rogue bubble of delight bounced round inside her before she reminded herself that not only did chivalry not exist in her world, she neither needed nor looked for it.

His brows snapped together. 'Where I come from men don't hit women.'

Something warm started to unfurl deep inside her. 'Where I come from no one hits anyone.' The Jacksons employed far more subtle tactics.

'He called you darling. You cried out and jerked back.'

Oh. She felt her cheeks grow warm. 'Well, yes, but only because I didn't want to get splashed,' she said. 'And Mark calls everyone darling.'

His hands sprang off her as if she were a hot coal and he stepped back. 'You didn't want to get splashed,' he echoed softly, his voice suddenly so cold and distant that it sent a chill hurtling down her spine and she automatically rubbed her upper arms.

In the thundering silence that hung between them, a seed of shame took root in her head and the blush on her cheeks deepened. His face was dark, tight and as hard as stone.

The combination of sheer disbelief and icy disdain that replaced the concern in his eyes made her wish she'd kept her mouth shut. If she'd kept her mouth shut she'd still be in his arms, enveloped in his heat and strength, feeling all warm and deliciously quivery instead of feeling as shallow as the pond and utterly rotten.

Then she rallied. Hang on a moment. Why was *she* being made to feel the guilty party in this little melodrama? She hadn't exactly begged him for help. And it was hardly her fault if he'd mistaken her dodging an arc of champagne for something more serious. While a spattering of water turned her sleek mane of hair into a frizzy mess, a carelessly flung spray of champagne would turn it into a frizzy *sticky* mess and she had enough to worry about right at this minute.

Phoebe nipped that seed of shame in the bud. 'This,' she said coolly, pointing at her hair, 'takes hours to straighten and my dress is dry-clean only.'

For a split second Alex looked dumbstruck and then his expression shuttered and his eyes went blank. She cast a glance over his hair, thick, dark and unfairly shiny. Of course he would never understand the struggle she had with her hair, nor the burning need to keep it under control. But what was his problem?

'Look, I didn't ask you to interfere,' she pointed out. 'And I certainly didn't need your help.'

'So I'm beginning to gather.'

'I had the situation totally under control.'

'You were standing barefoot with a twig in your hair and your dress hitched up around your hips—'

'Thighs,' she snapped. 'But wherever my dress was and whatever my hairstyle, you had no business interfering.'

Alex shoved his hands through his hair. 'What did you expect me to do? Stand back and watch you get hurt? Did you really think that he was going to come out willingly?'

Phoebe blinked. 'Well, yes.' With a little persuasion and guidance.

'In case you hadn't noticed, Mark is built like a tank and was totally out of control. Your lack of judgement astonishes me.'

Phoebe flinched. Ouch, that hurt. 'I wasn't in any danger,' she said. 'Mark was incapable of hitting anything. Anyway, what did you do with him?'

'I threw him out.'

Of course. 'Did anyone see you?'

He frowned. 'Does it matter?'

Phoebe gaped. *Did it matter?* She briefly wondered if steam actually whooshed out of her ears. 'Of course it matters.'

Alex let out a harsh incredulous laugh. 'You'd seriously put what other people think before your own safety? Your priorities are unbelievable.'

'My priorities are my own business. You,' she said, glaring at him, 'overreacted.'

Alex looked as if it was taking every ounce of his control not to wrap his hands round her throat and throttle her. 'Do you have *any* idea how volatile someone in that state can be? They can switch from charming to violent in the blink of an eye.' He leaned in so close that she could see her own image reflected in his eyes and snapped his fingers and she jumped. 'Just like that.'

Phoebe stamped down the stab of curiosity that suddenly demanded to know whether his reaction was based on personal experience of something similar and channelled her indignation instead. 'Look,' she said icily, 'this isn't the first time I've come across someone who can't handle his drink. Before you,' she said, stepping forwards, uncurling her fist and jabbing him in the chest with her index finger, 'barged in and started throwing Mark around like some sort of caveman everything was fine. I was dealing with it perfectly well. On my own.'

Phoebe broke off, breathing heavily, suddenly aware that Alex wasn't listening to her. His jaw was rigid. Colour slashed along his cheekbones. He was staring at her mouth, his big frame almost vibrating with an odd sort of electric tension.

She could feel his heart pounding beneath her hand. She could feel the scorching heat of his body burning through his shirt to singe her palm. She could feel his nipple, hot and tight, pressing against her hand.

Appal thundered through her. His heart? His heat? His nipple? *Beneath her hand?*

Her gaze shot down to the finger that had been poking his chest. Only now the jabbing had stopped. Now her hand lay flat against his chest and any minute now her fingers would be clutching at his shirt and yanking him towards her.

Time seemed to judder to a halt. Music drifted towards them, the sultry beat winding through her and whipping up unfamiliar sensations that stretched out and took over her ability to think about anything other than having his mouth hot and demanding on hers.

Phoebe could barely comprehend what was happening to her. No man had ever had this effect on her before. She'd felt attraction, tremors of lust even. Quite often. But never this slow drugging desire humming deep inside her, making her whole body itch with the need to reacquaint itself with his.

She wouldn't even have that far to tug. One centimetre. Maybe two. And they'd be locked together, tumbling down onto the pile of huge cushions that lined the pergola and pulling at each other's clothing.

In the middle of a party that she was supposed to be running.

With a sharp gasp of horror she snatched her hand away and took a hasty step back. Alex's eyes shot back up to hers. Dark, lit with something that made her mouth dry and her pulse hammer. 'No one saw me,' he said, the trace of huskiness in his voice telling her that an identical thought had been running through his head.

'Thank goodness for that,' she managed, although her throat felt like sandpaper. She ran the tip of her tongue over her lips and swallowed hard. 'Now I'd like an apology.'

'I'd like a thank you.'

Phoebe stuck her chin up and gave him a cool smile. 'Then I guess we're both destined to be disappointed.'

Alex reached out to slide his hand round to the small of her back and pulled her against him. 'Not necessarily.'

CHAPTER TWO

As HIS MOUTH slammed down on hers Phoebe instantly lost track of everything except for the flood of heat that rushed straight to the centre of her. He took advantage of her gasp of shock instantly. When their tongues met it was as if someone had lit a firework deep inside her and Phoebe couldn't do anything other than melt against him. Her arms shot up around his neck and his tightened and whether he pulled or she pushed, all she knew was that she was plastered against him and her body thought it had died and gone to heaven.

She ought to pull away. This was utter madness. She was supposed to be working. She'd planned every minute of this party, and at no stage did her plans involve six feet plus of devastating masculinity swooping to her unneeded rescue, kissing her and messing up her mind.

But tingles rippled along her nerve endings and the scent of him wound up her nose, seeped into her brain and fried it. All rational thought vanished.

As the kiss deepened and spiralled into something wildly out of control Phoebe felt the evidence of his arousal press against her and she wanted to writhe against it. Barely aware of what she was doing, she raised herself onto the tips of her toes to feel his hard length better against her, but her dress was too tight, too constricting.

Her breasts felt heavy and swollen and she wanted him to push the bodice down, get rid of her bra and soothe her aching nipples with his hand and mouth. When his hand moved round to cup her breast, lights exploded behind her eyelids and lust thundered through her.

Oh, God, she thought, beginning to tremble uncontrollably. She'd never been kissed like this. Had never kissed anyone like this. And she'd never been swept away by this intensity of...feeling.

'Phoebe?'

They both froze at the sound of Jo's voice. Phoebe let out a tiny moan of protest and Alex jerked back, cursing softly. She hung limply in his embrace and stared up at him in stunned silence. His hair was rumpled from where her fingers had tangled through it and a muscle pounded in his jaw. He seemed to be as shaken as she was. But a moment later he'd let her go and had backed into the shadows.

She blinked and swayed for a second while Jo called her name again, her voice louder and closer, and then reality swooped in and hit her round the head with the force of a fully laden tote bag.

What had she been *thinking?* She was at work. What if Jo hadn't called her name? She'd have come across the two of them practically devouring each other, which was most certainly *not* the sort of professionalism she prided herself on.

Desperately trying to regulate her breathing, Phoebe smoothed her dress and pressed the backs of her hands to her cheeks. As she suspected. Burning. She touched her still tingling mouth, which felt ravaged and bruised, and wondered exactly how bad the damage was.

'Hey, Phoebs, here you are.' Jo came to a halt at the entrance to the pergola and beamed. 'What are you doing out here all on your own?'

Phoebe resisted the urge to glance around to see where Alex had vanished to and cleared her throat. 'Oh, you know,' she said, smiling weakly while searching her imagination for something more sensible to say than an awestruck 'wow, did I just imagine that?'. 'Getting some air.'

Pathetic. She made her living out of manipulating words and spinning situations. Surely she could come up with something better than that?

'Hmm. It is a bit stuffy inside.' Jo frowned. 'What's happened to your hair?'

Oops, she'd forgotten all about that. Her hands shot to her head and she carefully pulled out her makeshift hairpin. She combed her fingers through her hair and thanked God that it appeared to have come through recent events unscathed.

Jo glanced down. 'What on earth is that?'

'A twig.'

'What was it doing in your hair?'

Phoebe tossed it into a flowerbed and waved a vague hand. 'Oh, I was simply experimenting with an idea.'

'Thinking of branching out?'

'Ha ha,' she muttered, and then clamped her lips together to stop a sudden bubble of hysterical laughter escaping.

Jo peered at her closer. 'Are you all right? You look a bit flushed. And flustered.' She paused and tilted her head. 'I've never seen you flustered.'

That was because she took great care never to appear

flustered, even when inside she was a mess. Regardless of the situation, triumph or disaster, she was always the epitome of cool, unflappable collectedness. She never let anything get in the way of her commitment to her job. And she never *ever* lost control.

Well, except for just now…

But that was totally understandable, she assured herself. After all, she'd been flung around like a sack of potatoes and then kissed senseless without any say in the matter whatsoever. Who wouldn't feel a tiny bit on the flustered side?

Phoebe took a deep breath and channelled her inner calm. 'I'm absolutely fine,' she said.

Jo shot her a knowing smile. 'If you weren't out here alone, and if I didn't know that you never mix business with pleasure, I'd have sworn I'd interrupted you in the middle of a clinch.'

Phoebe felt colour hit her cheeks and edged away from the light. It was high time to deflect this line of conversation. 'Hmm. So. You were looking for me?'

'Yes. I came to tell you…' But what Jo had come to tell her never made it out of her mouth.

Phoebe didn't need to look round to know that Alex was standing behind her. The hairs at the nape of her neck had leapt up like an early-warning system and her whole body quivered with awareness.

As Jo's gaze slid over Phoebe's shoulder her smile disappeared, the blood drained from her face and her eyes widened in horror.

'Hello, Jo.' Alex's voice was as cold as ice and Jo seemed to deflate right in front of Phoebe's eyes.

'Oh, no,' Jo said with a deep sigh. 'What are you doing here?'

* * *

Well, that was a relief, thought Alex darkly, thrusting his hands in his pockets and keeping his eyes fixed on his sister. Jo's reaction to his presence at the party was the only thing so far this evening that *had* turned out as he'd expected.

Ever since he'd learned that she'd gone behind his back and hired her own PR representative without his approval, he'd planned to pitch up, demand to know what she thought she was up to and replace whoever she'd hired with his own team.

He'd intended to swoop in and be done within a matter of minutes, and if things had gone according to plan, he'd now be passed out in his penthouse, battling jet lag.

Instead, over the course of the last half an hour he'd fought a drunken idiot in a pond, been thwacked by a deluge of painful memories he'd really rather forget and been forced to face the uncomfortable realisation that for the first time in years he'd been wrong. As if all that weren't enough, it appeared he'd also caught a severe case of lust.

Alex flicked a quick glance at Phoebe, standing there with her dark hair tumbling over her shoulders and looking like a fallen angel, and felt desire whip through him all over again.

Kissing the life out of one of the guests had definitely not been part of the plan. But the moment he'd held her against him he'd been able to think about little else. He could still feel the imprint of her hand on his chest while she'd been ranting about dealing with cavemen or something, her eyes flashing sparks of green and gold at him. When his resistance had finally crumbled she'd fitted against him so perfectly, responded to him so passionately that he hadn't been able to stop. Who knew what might have happened if Jo hadn't interrupted them?

Alex ground his teeth against the urge to drag Phoebe back into the shadows. There'd be plenty of time for that later. Once he'd achieved what he'd come here to do, he'd take her out to dinner. See where a few more of those kisses might end up and maybe find a new way to get over jet lag.

In the meantime, he told himself, blanking Phoebe from his head and training his full attention on Jo, he had work to do.

'Surprised to see me?' he said coolly.

'Somewhat,' Jo muttered. 'But thrilled too, of course,' she added hastily.

She didn't look in the slightest bit thrilled. She looked wary, as if she'd been caught red-handed. Which she should, because she had. If he'd vaguely entertained the idea of giving her the benefit of the doubt over the absence of his invitation, it vanished.

'Of course,' he replied dryly.

'How did you find out?'

'Did you really imagine I wouldn't?'

'I had hoped.'

Alex frowned. Since when had she started keeping secrets from him? That rankled almost as much as the fact that she'd deliberately kept him out of the loop.

'Er, excuse me for interrupting, but would someone mind telling me what's going on?' said Phoebe, edging towards Jo in an oddly protective fashion. 'Because I'm guessing you don't have an invitation, and, if Jo wants, I can have the bouncers here faster than you can say "gatecrasher."'

Alex's gaze swivelled back to his sister. 'Well?' he said in a deadly soft voice.

'There's no need to call the bouncers.' Jo pulled her shoulders back and shot him a defiant look. 'Alex, I'd like you to meet Phoebe Jackson, managing director of Jackson Communications, and my PR.'

Jo's words hit him with the force of a swinging boom and his blood turned to ice in his veins. He glanced at Phoebe, who was staring at him with a determined tilt of her chin and an arched eyebrow.

This was the woman he'd come to fire? The raven-haired goddess in the tight gold dress, who'd piqued his interest the second he'd laid eyes on her sneaking out of a side door? The woman he'd been imagining naked and warm and writhing in his arms? Something curiously like disappointment walloped him in the solar plexus. Alex rubbed his chest and frowned.

Then suspicion began to prickle at the edges of his brain. If she and his sister were working together had she colluded with her to deliberately keep him out of the proceedings? Even taking into account his natural mistrust of anyone and anything that he personally hadn't tested to the limit, it wasn't beyond the realm of possibility.

Whether she had or not, dinner was off. With the ruthless control he'd honed over the years, Alex crushed the lingering flickers of desire and stashed any attraction he felt towards Phoebe behind an unbreachable wall of icy neutrality.

Hmm, thought Phoebe, watching his whole body tense and sort of freeze. For some reason the news of her identity hadn't gone down well at all. Which was odd—she didn't normally incite such a violent reaction in people.

'And, Phoebe, this is Alex Gilbert. My brother.'

She was so busy trying to work out what objection he could possibly have to her that she almost missed Jo's words. But as they filtered into her head Phoebe found herself in the unusual position of being rendered speechless. And then a dozen little facts cascaded into her brain, each one hot on the heels of the other, and she inwardly groaned.

Oh, no.

How typical was that?

Someone really wanted this evening to implode. Because what were the chances that her mysterious, mind-blowingly gorgeous stranger would turn out to be the hotshot venture capitalist who'd injected a huge sum of cash so that Jo could finish and launch her collection? The billionaire who was so busy jetting round the world taking over businesses and entertaining glamorous women that he'd refused the invitation.

She hated it when she was wrong-footed. And not just wrong-footed. Hurled off balance would be a more accurate description. She'd swooned in his arms. Melted against him. Practically devoured him, for heaven's sake. How mortifyingly inappropriate was that?

'I should have guessed,' she said hiding her embarrassment behind a cool façade. 'The family resemblance is uncanny.'

She might be burning up inside, but Alex didn't appear to be the slightest bit fazed. 'Technically I'm her half-brother,' he said with an impersonal little smile. 'We shared a mother and we each take after our fathers.' He held out a hand. Phoebe felt an arc of electricity shoot up her arm when her palm hit his and had to force herself not to snatch it back.

What was he doing here anyway? Jo had said he was quite content to be a silent partner. That he had no interest in what Jo got up to and even less in handbags.

When she'd heard about his supposed lack of fraternal support it hadn't surprised her in the slightest. After all, when had *her* siblings ever supported her? At least he'd shown up at the eleventh hour, which was more than she could expect from any member of her family, all of whom thought her choice of career unbelievably frivolous.

Well, frivolous it might be, but it had given her enough experience to handle any situation with sophistication and aplomb. Even one as awkward as this.

'I thought you were supposed to be in the States,' she said evenly.

'I was.'

'Venturing your capital?'

'Negotiating a deal.'

'Did you win?'

'He always wins,' said Jo grumpily.

'I'm sure you do,' she said smoothly, pulling her hand out of his and surreptitiously flexing her fingers to stop the tingling. 'Anyway, naturally we're delighted to see you.'

'Really?' he said raising an eyebrow. 'In that case, I can only imagine my invitation got lost in the post.'

Phoebe frowned. 'You refused it.'

'Did I?' he said flatly, his expression turning even stonier.

'You were obviously too busy to remember refusing it as well as being too busy to come.'

'Obviously,' he drawled and somehow Phoebe instantly knew that he'd been nothing of the kind.

'So why the change of heart? A hitherto unrecognised fascination for women's accessories?'

A slow smouldering smile curved his lips, and she felt herself heating up. 'This is my little sister's debut. How could I possibly miss it?'

'Then why refuse in the first place?' Something wasn't right here, but for the life of her Phoebe couldn't work out what. Alex had turned her brain to mush.

'All right,' said Jo, throwing her hands up in the air. 'Phoebe, Alex knows perfectly well that I never sent him an invitation.'

Now she was baffled. Phoebe blinked and swung her attention back to Jo. 'So why did you tell me you had?'

'Oh, I really don't remember,' said Jo vaguely, waving a hand.

'Forgetfulness seems to run in the family,' Phoebe said dryly, not believing her for a second. Jo had been very unforthcoming about her brother, despite the fact that he'd contributed so much to her fledgling career, and now that she thought about it Phoebe realised that whenever she'd mentioned the financial generosity of Jo's elusive brother, Jo had deftly changed the subject, which she'd thought odd at the time. However Phoebe had enough experience of tricky sibling relationships to steer well clear of other people's and hadn't probed.

With hindsight, she should have insisted on knowing more. His name at least. That would have saved her a whole lot of trouble.

'Anyway, you two should get to know each other.'

No, they shouldn't. Phoebe already knew far more about Alex than she was comfortable with, and his rigid expression gave her the impression that he wasn't particularly keen on the idea either.

'We met earlier,' she said pleasantly. 'The encounter was brief.'

'But intense,' he said, shooting her a searing look.

'And wet, by the looks of things,' said Jo, frowning as she glanced at the damp patches on Alex's suit.

'I decided to take a stroll round the gardens. It involved an unexpected detour via the pond.' Alex rubbed his chest and Phoebe was instantly transported back to the moments before he'd kissed her. Images flashed into her head. The way he'd stared at her mouth, the hunger in his expression and the fire in his eyes. So different from the cold, controlled man standing in front of her.

Surely he couldn't be that upset about not being sent an invitation? But if it wasn't that, what was it?

'If you're falling into ponds,' said Jo lightly, 'you must be more jet-lagged than usual.'

'I must be,' murmured Alex. His eyes locked with Phoebe's and her stomach flipped.

'Jet lag makes him do the oddest things,' said Jo, clearly thankful that the attention had shifted away from her. 'The last time he had it he shredded a six-figure cheque instead of banking it and stashed his car keys in the fridge.'

Phoebe raised an eyebrow. 'How absolutely fascinating.'

'Don't you just love siblings?' he drawled.

'Simply adore them,' she said, and then thought of her own. 'But I couldn't eat a whole one.'

He didn't even crack a smile and Phoebe felt her hackles shoot up. What was his problem? 'I didn't think international playboys bothered with things like fridges.'

A warning gleam entered his eyes. 'Are you making assumptions about me, Phoebe?'

'Simply making an observation,' she said with an innocent smile.

'Champagne has to be chilled somewhere, don't you think?'

'It certainly does. The colder the better.'

'Especially in this heat.'

Phoebe shivered at the smouldering silvery sparks in his gaze.

'It's not that warm,' said Jo. 'Not for May. And, Phoebs, you've got goose-bumps.'

'Cold?' Alex asked softly, running his gaze over her, and to her irritation her body responded instantly. Her breasts tightened uncomfortably against the close-fitting dress and her nipples hardened while hot flames of desire licked deep inside her.

'No.'

The seconds stretched, and the longer their gazes held, the more it felt as if nothing else existed beyond the sizzling attraction that arced between them. Her gaze dipped to his mouth and the desperate longing to have it on hers again thumped her in the stomach.

And Alex wanted it too, she realised with a jolt. She could tell by the darkening of his eyes and by the way his body seemed to go utterly still. Phoebe shuddered at the desire that suddenly ripped through her and dragged in a shaky breath. Alex frowned and ran a hand through his hair and when he jerked his attention away from her Phoebe felt as if a piece of elastic had snapped her in the face.

She had to stop this. She'd never had trouble controlling her hormones before, so why now?

Jo thankfully seemed oblivious to the electric undercurrents that fizzed between them and was looking round the gardens. 'So what do you think of the venue?' she asked brightly. 'Isn't it heavenly?'

'Quite literally, given that we're six storeys above the streets of central London,' Alex replied. 'The gardens are…' his gaze swung back to Phoebe and her heart practically thudded to a halt '…illuminating.'

'That'll be the clever lighting,' she said, amazed that her voice sounded so steady when her whole body was trembling.

'Not that clever if you're falling into ponds. By the way, have either of you seen Mark?'

Alex tensed. 'Who's Mark?'

'My new boyfriend.' Jo beamed.

Alex's jaw clenched and his face darkened.

'I've been looking all over the place for him but can't find him anywhere. I thought he might have come out here.'

'He did.'

There was a heavy silence. And then eventually Jo swung round, and stared at him. 'Oh no. Have you met him?' She frowned, her expression starting out wary but then when Alex didn't answer immediately, turning to anger. 'What happened? What did you do to him?'

Alex's face was as rigid as stone and Phoebe hoped she'd never give him cause to look at her like that. With all that restrained strength and power, combined with the scar and the bump on his nose, she had a feeling Alex Gilbert could be a dangerous man to cross. 'I poured him into a taxi and sent him home.'

'I don't believe it,' said Jo, her voice tense with frustration. 'Why did you do that?'

'Mark was slightly the worse for wear,' Phoebe interjected. 'I tried to persuade him to cool off but he wasn't really co-operating.'

'Mark was off his head,' Alex corrected sharply, 'and

I was under the brief misapprehension that Phoebe's safety was at stake.'

Jo's mouth dropped open. 'Why would her safety be at stake?

'I thought he'd hit her,' he said flatly.

'Oh,' said Jo in a small voice.

A look passed between Alex and his sister that Phoebe couldn't identify and that nugget of shame threatened to resprout inside her. 'Nevertheless,' said Phoebe, forcing it down, 'you overreacted.'

'We've already been through that,' grated Alex.

'I could put it down to jet lag if you'd like,' said Phoebe helpfully, and then shuddered at the dark scowl that crossed his face.

Jo sighed and her shoulders slumped. 'Was Mark very drunk?'

'As a skunk,' said Phoebe, 'and after some time in the pond he smelt a bit like one too.'

Jo's nose wrinkled. 'What was he doing in the pond?'

'Making friends with the wildlife,' said Alex dryly. 'Someone forgot to put up a fence.'

'No one forgot,' said Phoebe. 'It's deliberate. It's cool. The fencelessness of the San Lorenzo Roof Gardens symbolises the uninhibited harmony between man and nature, and is part of its uber-cool appeal.' At least that was what the website claimed.

'It's absurd,' Alex growled. 'Your boyfriend,' he said, emphasising the word with sharp disdain as his gaze skewered Jo to the spot, 'could have caused serious damage.'

'It's not his fault,' said Jo, her face falling. 'He's up to his ears in debt.'

'Idiot,' muttered Alex.

'Spoken like a true billionaire,' said Phoebe tartly.

Alex's eyes glittered dangerously. 'There you go again,' he said, shaking his head as if in disappointment. 'Jumping to conclusions and making rash assumptions. I haven't always been a billionaire. I know what it's like to have nothing but debts.'

So do I, thought Phoebe, and tried not to think about the enormous loan she'd taken out to set up her business.

'But I didn't drown myself in drink,' Alex added.

'Lucky you.' There were times when Phoebe felt like mainlining vodka, but so far she'd managed to resist.

He turned to Jo. 'I don't think you should see him again.'

'Thanks to you I probably won't,' Jo fired back.

Right. Phoebe had had enough of this. Sibling squabbling had no place here. 'Perhaps you two could continue this discussion another time,' she said in a voice that brooked no argument. 'Jo, you need to go back inside and mingle. Alex, you need to get a drink and relax. And I need to get on with making sure nothing else goes wrong.'

'Ms Jackson?'

Phoebe spun round to see the portly form of Mr Bogoni barrelling towards them, huffing and puffing and looking as if he were on the verge of exploding. Her spirits dipped at the expression on his face. Oh, Lord. What was the matter now? Surely one mishap was quite enough for one evening.

'Ms Jackson,' he said again, smoothing his hair.

'Mr Bogoni,' said Phoebe, flashing him a bright smile that as usual didn't manage to dent the icy demeanour. 'You'll be delighted to know that the flamingo remains unharmed.'

'I am indeed glad to hear that, but unfortunately we have another problem.'

'What sort of problem?'

'I think you'd better come with me.'

CHAPTER THREE

PHOEBE'S MIND RACED as she followed Mr Bogoni across the terrace towards the bar. What could possibly have happened now? And why did Alex have to be following quite so closely? In fact why did he have to be there at all? 'There was no need for you to come too,' Phoebe muttered out of the side of her mouth.

'You think not?' he drawled. 'This is perhaps the most important night of my sister's career. I'm interested in everything that goes on.'

'Whatever it is,' said Jo firmly, 'Phoebe will be able to fix it.'

Phoebe shot Jo a smile of thanks for her vote of confidence and prepared herself for the worst.

But as she stepped into the bar her eyes were drawn up and she froze in absolute horror.

Oh, dear God. This wasn't a problem. This was a disaster of gargantuan proportions, the likes of which nothing in her experience could have prepared her for. Compared to this, the Mark debacle was as insignificant as a tiny sequin on a full-length ball gown.

Phoebe blinked to check she wasn't hallucinating, but no. This was no hallucination.

Every single one of Jo's beautiful handbags was on fire. Multicoloured flames licked at the precious creations and the acrid smell of burning plastic and fabric filled the room. Sparks flew. Metal crackled. Then, as if cremating handbags weren't bad enough, the individual light above each pedestal went out, the localised sprinkler system kicked in and tiny droplets of water rained over the charred remains. Smoke billowed and then whooshed up into the powerful air conditioning vents.

Icy panic flooded through her. How on earth was she going to spin this? All the guests had edged to the sides of the room and every single one of them was staring up at the spectacle in utter amazement. Jo looked as if she was on the verge of tears; Alex's stony expression told her he wasn't amused in the slightest.

The dreadful silence gave way to a rumble of speculation that began to sweep through the room. Gasps of amazement were swiftly followed by murmurs about flammable fabric and toxic materials and Phoebe realised that if she didn't do something in the next few minutes the situation would become unsalvageable and her business would fail barely before it had begun.

But what? For the first time in her life, she didn't have a clue what to say. Terror clawed at her chest and a ball of panic lodged in her throat. Her head went fuzzy and for a moment she thought she was about to start hyperventilating.

No. She didn't have time to hyperventilate. Not when Jo's bags had all just exploded like firecrackers.

Phoebe's heart skipped a beat. Wait a moment… firecrackers…

The idea that popped into her head was so outrageously crazy, so unbelievable, that it might actually work. It was a gamble, but if she showed she believed it, everyone else would too, and she'd have turned a major disaster into a fabulous finale.

Euphoric relief wiped the fuzz from her head and an unstoppable grin spread across her face. 'Don't worry about a thing,' she said, leaning over to whisper in Jo's ear and giving her arm a reassuring squeeze. 'It's all going to be fine.'

So how was she going to wriggle out of this one?

Alex leaned against a pillar and folded his arms over his chest as Phoebe marched across the empty floor, stepped up onto the dais and tapped the microphone. All eyes watched her and the room filled with a sort of morbid excitement that reminded him of birds of prey circling an injured animal.

How could Jo ever have thought that hiring someone of her own accord was a wise thing to do? Especially someone who allowed the evening to descend into chaos.

As far as he was aware his sister knew nothing about PR. Whereas he'd worked with his team for years. So why hadn't she come to him and asked for his advice on something so important? Alex ignored the twinge of hurt and made himself pay attention to what Phoebe was about to say.

'Ladies and gentlemen,' she began, smiling broadly and waiting until every drop of focus was on her. 'Rockets… Catherine wheels… Sparklers… And now handbags.' She paused. 'I think you'll all agree that our grand pyrotechnical finale was much more original than a firework display. A little earlier than planned, perhaps, but no less spectacular.'

Alex's jaw tightened. Hah. She was doomed. As if

anyone was going to believe a story as ridiculous as that. With one ear on the rest of her speech, which continued in the same dubious vein, he surveyed the room with a sceptical eye. She'd never pull this off.

He was just beginning to congratulate himself on having saved Jo from a terrible career move, when to his utter amazement people began to smile and nod and whisper to each other. Surely people couldn't actually be buying her absurd explanation?

'And as that rounds off the evening's events,' Phoebe said finally, 'I'd like to thank you all for coming, and hope you enjoy the upcoming launch of the debut collection of the fabulous Jo Douglas.'

Jo stepped up to her side and gave a little curtsey. Phoebe started clapping and as everyone else joined in the sound grew into a thunderous applause. The pair of them stepped off the dais, basking in glory, and Alex watched through narrowed eyes as a woman in purple cornered Phoebe and a crowd of people flocked around Jo.

OK, so that was a clever wiggle, he grudgingly admitted, still slightly stunned by the fact that everyone had apparently bought into her explanation. Her timing was impeccable, her imagination was extraordinary and she'd had her audience eating out of her hand.

Maybe Phoebe wasn't as incapable as he'd originally thought, but that was tough. To his mind she was an enigma and that made her a liability. And what did Jo really know about her anyway? He'd bet everything he had that she hadn't delved that far into her background and her experience, and had made little effort to see whether she was trustworthy. So it was lucky he'd shown up when he did.

Gradually the guests drifted off and Jo bounded over

to him, grinning like a lunatic. 'You see,' she said triumphantly. 'I told you Phoebe'd fix it. Isn't she amazing?'

Alex grimaced. Amazing wasn't quite the word he'd use to describe her. Beautiful. That was a good one. Sexy as hell. With a mouth that had been made for kissing and a body that seemed to have been created specially to fit to his.

The kiss they'd shared beneath the pergola slammed into his head and a savage kick of lust thumped him in the gut.

Damn. Burying his attraction to her was going to take far more effort than he'd thought. Still, once he'd got rid of her, desire would fade and in future he'd steer well clear of women who obliterated his self-control and drove him mindless with just a kiss.

'Why didn't you tell me you were planning to hire someone to do your PR?' he said mildly, his voice betraying nothing of the battle raging inside him.

'Because I knew you wouldn't have approved.'

'You're right. I don't. I want you to use my PR people.'

Jo sighed. 'You see. *This* is why I didn't want you here. I knew you were going to do this. Alex, I don't want to use your people.'

'Why not? My team are tried and tested. Reliable.' At least as reliable as anyone other than himself could be.

Jo's expression turn mutinous and Alex wondered where this backbone of steel had sprung from. 'Your team might be excellent at dealing with finance and inventions and things, but they wouldn't know one end of a handbag from the other.' Alex felt his jaw tighten. That might be true, but they could learn. 'Phoebe handled the account of a graduate from my college a few years ago when she was working at one of the big PR agencies.

Maria now works in Paris for one of the top fashion houses. Phoebe has incredible contacts and, well, you can see for yourself what she's achieved this evening.'

Alex let out a short burst of incredulous laughter. As far as he could tell, all she'd achieved was a series of disasters.

Jo shifted her weight from one foot to the other, but didn't look as if she intended to back down. 'OK, so I admit that my handbags on fire wasn't exactly in the plans, but would your PR team have come up with such a spectacular excuse?'

Probably not, but that wasn't the point. 'My PR team would never have let it happen in the first place.'

'Phoebe didn't "let" it happen. It was an accident. Not even you can turn it into her fault.'

Hmm. Pity. The implication of her words sank in and Alex winced. He wasn't that unreasonable. If he did come over as heavy-handed occasionally it was only for Jo's benefit. But his sister clearly didn't see it like that. In her eyes Phoebe could do little wrong. Knowing which battles to fight if he wanted to win, Alex decided to switch tactics. 'How well do you know her?'

'Pretty well. I've been working with her for two months.'

Two months was nothing. He'd known Rob for ten years and it hadn't stopped his best friend betraying him. 'And how do you know she won't drop you the moment someone with better prospects comes along?'

Jo sighed. 'At the moment I'm her only client. She needs me as much as I need her so I think that makes her pretty trustworthy, don't you?' She pushed a lock of hair off her face and fixed him with a stare. 'Look, Alex. I know I've been a nightmare and have given you untold cause for worry. And you'll never know how grateful I am for all the help and support you've given me but I really need to start taking responsibility for my own life. Mistakes and all. You can't keep protecting me for ever.'

Couldn't he? He'd been doing exactly that ever since her parents died and he didn't intend to stop now. Especially after the hideous events of five years ago when he'd screwed up so spectacularly. A familiar wave of guilt washed over him and his chest tightened. He didn't intend to screw up again.

'Alex, I really want this. Phoebe and I work well together. She understands what I need. Please don't mess this up for me.'

The quiet pleading in her voice cut right through him and Alex felt his resolve waver. He ran his gaze over her and looked at her properly for the first time this evening. She'd changed in the two months since he'd last seen her. She seemed more confident, more determined, healthier. More like the girl she'd been before she'd met Rob.

Alex sighed and felt his control over her well-being begin to slip away. As harrowing as the prospect of letting Jo find her own way in the world was, maybe she was right. She was twenty-two. He couldn't protect her for ever. Maybe it was time he loosened the reins. A little. But if either of them thought he'd just sit back and hope for the best, they could think again.

CHAPTER FOUR

By eleven o'clock the following morning Phoebe had spent three hours at her desk, poring over the press, answering calls from potential clients and trying not to wonder where Alex had disappeared to the night before.

Maybe he'd had a date. Maybe he'd succumbed to jet lag and had crashed out in a flowerbed. Maybe he'd been appalled by the haphazard way the party had panned out and left in disgust.

Who knew? Jo certainly hadn't. And Phoebe really oughtn't to care either way; as a silent partner he was unlikely to be popping up all the time, and as her client's brother—and therefore strictly off limits—he could date whoever and pass out wherever he chose. Not that he'd ever been *on* limits, of course.

But to her intense irritation she did care. Because regardless of where Alex had physically got to last night, he was now lodged in her head and she was going slowly out of her mind.

Her memory had become photographic where Alex was concerned. Every detail of his dark handsome face, every inch of his incredible body was as clear as if he were standing in front of her and she just couldn't get rid of the image, no matter how hard she tried.

Phoebe pinched the bridge of her nose and screwed her eyes up. He had no right invading her thoughts like this. It was bad enough that he'd barged into her dreams and had proceeded to do all sorts of deliciously erotic things to her that had woken her up hot and sweating and pulsating with need.

Sleep had whisked her back to the pergola, where he'd kissed her over and over again until she'd been panting and whimpering. Only this time, nothing had interrupted them and Alex had slid down the zip of her dress and peeled it off her and then his hands had stroked over her skin, before pulling her down with him onto the cushions and—

Agh. Phoebe jumped to her feet, utterly disgusted with her lack of control over something so primitive, and marched into the kitchen.

She needed a cup of coffee. So what if she'd already had five? Number six would sort her out. It had to. Otherwise she'd never last the morning.

The phone rang just as she was pouring water into the cafetiere. Her hand jerked and boiling water splashed her skin.

Phoebe howled in pain and frustration. This edginess was so unlike her. Whenever stress threatened to wipe her out, all she usually had to do was take a series of deep breaths and channel the serenity of her office. But today those yoga techniques, the acres of bare white walls and the ordered tranquillity of her surroundings weren't working.

Scowling and rubbing her hand, Phoebe inhaled deeply, closed her eyes and forced herself to pick up the phone slowly and calmly. 'Hello?' Good. Pleasant and polite. That didn't sound bad.

'Phoebs, I have an Alex Gilbert in Reception.'

Phoebe dropped the phone and watched helplessly as it bounced twice and then skidded across the floor-boards. So much for inner calm.

What was he doing here? Had her fevered imagination actually conjured him up? What did he want?

'Phoebs? Are you there?'

Oh, to be able to yell 'no!' and go and hide under her desk. But the opportunity to imitate her answer machine and pretend she was out had long gone. 'Just a moment,' she called and dashed across the floor to where her phone lay.

Phoebe picked up the handset. Then she straightened her suit and smoothed her hair and dredged up every ounce of self-possession she had. 'Thanks, Lizzie,' she said serenely. 'You'd better tell him to come up.'

All she had to do was remain steady and in control and everything would be fine.

Alex glanced around Phoebe's office and felt like fishing out his sunglasses. Apart from the woman in the severe black trouser suit perched against the edge of the sparkling glass desk and a few certificates and pictures hanging on the walls everything was blindingly white.

'Good morning, Alex.'

She looked so composed with her poker straight hair and aloof air that for an insane moment he wanted to ruffle her up. 'Good morning, Phoebe.'

'Coffee?'

'No, thank you.'

'Did you have a pleasant evening?'

'Delightful.' And busy. Once he'd reluctantly given in to Jo, he'd gone back to his apartment, had formulated a plan and had wasted no time in setting the wheels in motion.

'I'm so glad.' She gave him a chilly smile and moved round to the other side of her desk. She gestured to the chair on his side. 'Please. Do sit down.'

'Thank you.' Alex folded himself onto the perspex chair and sat back.

'How's the jet lag?'

'Fine.'

'Shredded any cheques?'

Alex grinned. 'Not so far. How are the handbags?'

'Ruined beyond repair.'

'Whose idea was it to put them so close to the lights?'

'That would be mine.'

'Clever.'

She flinched and her eyes flashed. Perhaps she wasn't so composed after all, Alex thought with an odd sense of reassurance. After the heat and passion of last night, this morning's ultra-cool Phoebe had been faintly unnerving.

'I was led to believe that everything would be fine. The three risk assessments I carried out back me up. You can have a look at them if you'd like.'

Alex ignored her sarcasm. 'Any idea what happened?'

'According to the manager, someone had installed the wrong kind of light bulbs, and according to Jo she used highly flammable glue as a sort of quick fix in order to get some samples finished for last night. Normally she stitches everything by hand. A most unfortunate coincidence.'

'So it would seem.'

'Still, it wasn't all bad. Self-igniting accessories are apparently tipped to be the latest craze.'

'Extraordinary.'

Phoebe shrugged. 'Anything's possible in PR.' She picked up a pen and pulled a notepad towards her. 'Anyway,' she said with a bright smile that didn't reach her eyes, 'what do you want?'

Alex stretched his legs out and regarded her carefully. 'I have a proposition for you.'

That surprised her. 'Oh?'

'I'm hosting a party tomorrow night for colleagues and clients and a few friends. I want you to be there.'

Curiosity cracked the glacial façade. 'In what capacity?'

'I want you to raise money for one of the charities I support.'

Phoebe's eyes narrowed. 'That's not really what I do.'

He knew that, and that was the beauty of his test. 'Don't you want the business?' he said shooting her a shrewd glance.

Phoebe frowned. 'Naturally your offer is intriguing, but isn't raising money at a private party a little inappropriate?'

'Highly. There lies the challenge.'

'But why would you want to offer me a challenge?'

Alex regarded her thoughtfully for a while. 'Would you like to know the real reason I was at the party last night?'

Phoebe tensed. 'I'd be fascinated.'

'I came to fire you,' he said lazily.

Outside, traffic rumbled. Horns beeped. People shouted. But inside her office heavy silence descended.

Phoebe blinked and stared at him in disbelief. 'You know, for a moment there I thought you'd said you'd come to fire me.'

'I did.'

Phoebe went white for a second and then that brittle little smile snapped back to her face and Alex was struck by a sudden uncontrollable urge to wipe it away with a kiss. 'That's insane. I don't work for you so how can you fire me?'

He ignored the urge and kept his gaze well away from her mouth. 'I own sixty per cent of Jo's company. I can do whatever I like.'

Phoebe glowered. 'I thought you were supposed to be a silent partner.'

'I was.'

'Your particular brand of silence is deafening.' She paused and total bafflement swept across her face. 'Why would you want to fire me?' Then she frowned. 'Is this about the kiss?'

Alex started. 'Why would this be about the kiss?'

'Well, some might say there was a conflict of interest,' she muttered, taking an intense interest in the papers on her desk as her cheeks went pink.

'I didn't know who you were. Did you know who I was?'

'No. Jo barely mentioned you, and then never by name.'

'There'd only be a conflict of interest were I to kiss you now.'

Her head snapped up and the colour on her cheeks deepened. 'Er, quite.'

'And that's not going to happen.'

'Good,' she said sharply, as if she was trying to convince herself as much as him. 'Excellent.'

Was that disappointment that flared in her eyes? Alex shifted in the chair. 'So in answer to your question, no, my decision to fire you had nothing to do with the kiss.'

'What did it have to do with, then?'

'Your competency.'

Phoebe reeled. Her competency? What on earth was going on?

When Alex had informed her that he'd intended to fire her as casually as if they'd been discussing the weather, she'd thought that nothing more he said could shock her.

She'd been wrong.

'My competency?' He nodded. 'What about it?'

'Based on the…unusual…events of last night, I'm not convinced you're the best person to represent Jo.'

Phoebe gasped. The arrogance of the man. How dared he question her competency when he knew next to nothing about her? 'That's absurd.'

'Is it?' he said in that lazy drawl that made her want to thump him.

'Were you not there last night? Did you not see how I turned a fiasco into a triumph?' Phoebe glared at him, all hope of remaining polite and pleasant a dim and distant memory. 'Last night's party resulted in thirty column inches across six newspapers and four requests for interviews with Jo. Three magazines are going to run features on her and her handbags and the party will appear on the society pages in all of them. This morning I had a call from one of the major high street stores who want her to design a range of accessories for them.'

Phoebe got to her feet, as if standing would somehow stop her anger from brimming over and making her say something she might really regret. 'How, exactly, is that incompetent?'

Alex didn't answer. He merely raised an eyebrow and it shot her anger into incandescence. 'I'm very good at my job, Alex. I have ten years of experience. I've handled million-pound accounts and I've launched products that have turned into best-sellers. I'm also brilliant at breaking up rowing journalists at press conferences, evading difficult questions and managing crises. Winning over disapproving brothers is a new one for me, but I *will* get there in the end.' She paused and gave him an icy smile. 'I've been working with Jo for weeks and we make a great team. She has extraordinary potential and a great career ahead of her. Her launch is in a fortnight and all the plans are in place. I will not let you ruin this for her.'

Long seconds passed before Alex spoke and when he did his voice froze her blood. 'Why don't you tell me about the parts of your career that haven't, I presume, gone quite according to plan?'

The parts of her career that hadn't gone according to plan? His words whipped the wind from her sails and she dragged in a shaky breath. What parts? There weren't any. At least none that he could possibly know about... 'What do you mean?' she hedged, sitting back down and filling with trepidation.

The way he just looked at her, like an animal stalking its prey, turned her even colder. 'I'm talking about the soap, the perfume and the musician.'

Phoebe felt as if he'd pulled the chair out from underneath her. 'How do you know about them?'

Alex's eyes glittered. 'I know an awful lot about you.'

Her stomach fell away and her head went fuzzy. 'Did you have me investigated?'

Alex nodded.

'Why would you do that?'

'Standard due diligence procedures. Why wouldn't I?'

Phoebe rubbed her temples and sank back down into

her chair. Oh, God. He'd had her investigated? What sort of man did something like that? Jo had mentioned that Alex could be a touch on the protective side, but this was madness. Last night he hadn't even known her name. Now, thanks to investigators who must have toiled throughout the night, he probably knew more about her than she did herself.

'Unless you want me to fire you right now, you can start with the soap.' Alex's eyes glittered, as if he was actually relishing the moment.

Phoebe felt as if she were sitting on knives. 'What do you know about the soap?'

He gave her a mocking smile. 'You said that it brought out a rash and made your skin itch. To a journalist.'

'I didn't know he was a journalist. He bought me a drink. And another. And another. I thought he was being friendly.'

His mouth twisted. 'My point precisely.'

Phoebe sighed and rubbed her neck. How lucky she'd had plenty of practice justifying what she did, the decisions she'd taken and the mistakes she'd made. Compared to the grilling her family gave her on a monthly basis, this was a walk in the park.

But then, her family didn't hold her future in their hands.

Phoebe gathered her wits. She needed every drop of strength because right now she had to fight harder than she had in a long time.

'Alex, I was twenty-one. It was right at the beginning of my career. In the second week of my first job. I was naïve. I learnt.' She paused. 'Besides, it *did* give me a rash and make my skin itch. As a result they went back and tweaked the formula.'

'Nevertheless it was hardly a stellar moment.'

'I'm well aware of that.'

'And then what about the perfume?' He paused. 'Falsifying sales figures? I'd say that was verging on criminal.'

Phoebe stiffened. 'It was nothing of the kind. It was simply a mistake. I was given the wrong data.'

'And you didn't think to check?'

'I trusted my team.'

Alex grunted. 'Now *that* was a mistake,' he said more sharply than she would have thought the point warranted.

'Evidently. But you needn't worry. Now I check and double-check everything.'

Alex didn't look as if that information alleviated his concerns in the slightest.

So two blips down, only one remained. Phoebe's heart rate picked up. She'd spent so long in denial over this particular incident that she really didn't want to have to rake through it all over again. But she doubted Alex would let it rest.

'And the musician?'

She sighed and pinched the bridge of her nose and forced back the anguish that clenched her heart. 'Dillon Black was an up and coming musician looking for representation.' She shrugged as if the whole sorry affair had been a mere inconvenience instead of the heart-wrenching nightmare it had become. 'I signed him up with the company I was working for at the time.'

'I thought you specialised in fashion PR.'

Phoebe shifted on the chair and bit her lip. 'I do. That was the trouble. When someone with more experience offered him a better deal he jumped ship faster than you can say "recording label."'

'So why did you sign him up?'

Phoebe closed her eyes briefly. 'It was a blip. A one-off error of judgement.'

A tiny smile hovered over his mouth. 'So it had nothing to do with the fact that you were living together at the time?'

Phoebe's gaze jerked to his and her heart thundered. 'How do you know that?'

'My investigators are very thorough.'

'This is outrageous.'

Alex shrugged. 'Your lack of judgement seems to have been a recurrent theme in the course of your career.'

Phoebe gasped. How did he do that? He hit her where she was most vulnerable and then stuck the knife in, twisting it and slicing her heart open and releasing all the old aches and hurt.

'I wanted to help him,' she said, trying to keep a steady grip on her voice. 'I trusted him. I never imagined he'd turn around and betray me.'

Phoebe's heart hardened. She'd been so besotted by Dillon, had even thought herself in love with him, and he'd just been using her. Infatuation had made her take her eye off the ball, distracted her and screwed up her judgement. She'd very nearly lost her job and she'd vowed then and there that she'd never let herself get in that position again.

'More fool you,' he said flatly.

'Indeed. Anyway,' she said, pulling herself together and giving Alex a cool stare, 'you can be sure that my judgement is now well and truly back on track. The experience taught me, one, to stick with what I'm good at, two, not to allow anyone or anything to deflect my focus.'

So she'd made mistakes. Who hadn't? At least she'd

learned from them. Alex was probably the sort who never admitted to making a mistake. Never admitted to being wrong. Typical, she thought with a little sniff.

'Easy to say,' he said sharply.

Phoebe shot him a questioning glance. 'What's made you so deeply suspicious of people's behaviour?'

Alex's eyelids dropped slightly so she couldn't see the expression in his eyes. 'Experience.'

'Such cynicism in one so young.'

'Not that young.'

'Early thirties?'

'Thirty-two.'

'And in those thirty-two years, have you never made a mistake?'

'We're talking about you.'

Aha. So he had made a mistake. 'What was it, Alex?'

Alex's face darkened. 'For someone who's supposed to be fighting to keep their job, you're veering way off course.'

That was something else that she'd been wondering about. 'Why do you have responsibility over who Jo works with? She's twenty-two. Why can't she make her own decisions?'

His lips thinned. 'She can't be trusted to make her own decisions.'

Phoebe bristled. His arrogance was simply unbeliev-able. 'Why not?'

'Because she's made lousy decisions in the past.'

Haven't we all? thought Phoebe darkly. 'But surely they're her lousy decisions?'

Alex raked a hand through his hair and when he looked at her his expression was so desolate that Phoebe's heart clenched. 'Not when I have to pick up the pieces.'

'Why do you have to pick up the pieces?' Phoebe had always picked up her own pieces. Didn't everyone?

'I'm her brother.'

A tiny dart of envy pierced her chest, but she brushed it aside. 'Does she know you trust her judgement so little?'

'She knows I have her best interests at heart,' he said flatly.

'Her best interests at the moment are me.'

'Then accept the challenge.'

Phoebe sat back and tried to read his expression. But it gave away nothing other than the fact that his position on the matter was totally immutable.

'What if I say no? That I, for one, trust her judgement?'

'I would have no hesitation in replacing you with my own PR team.'

'Yours? Do they have any experience in fashion?'

'Not yet.'

Phoebe stared at him, unable to fathom the emotion in his eyes. 'You'd really do that? Even if it goes against Jo's wishes?'

'I would.'

'And even though I'm the best person for the job?'

She could practically hear his teeth grinding. 'All I want is what's best for her.'

No, he didn't, Phoebe realised with a flash of perception. Well, yes, the chances were he did want what was best for his sister, but that wasn't all. For some reason Alex wanted, needed, to stay in control.

In all probability he'd confronted Jo with his intention, and based on the interaction between the two of them she'd witnessed last night she'd bet her brand new pair of designer heels that Jo had retaliated. That must have frustrated the hell out of him.

Good.

Phoebe itched with the urge to tell him to get lost. But she couldn't. She had no doubt whatsoever that if she chose not to comply he'd have no compunction in batting her to one side and installing his own team. Aside from wrecking Jo's future, it would batter her professional pride and would have devastating consequences on her career.

She really *really* needed to hang onto Jo. If she lost her... Phoebe shuddered at the thought and felt a trickle of cold sweat ripple down her back. The bank would call in the loan, her business would collapse and she'd have failed before she'd barely got started.

Well, that was *not* going to happen. She wouldn't fail. She couldn't fail. Her family didn't do failure. Ever. And she didn't intend to be the one to break the mould.

So she'd accept his challenge, and win.

'I won't let her down,' she said with steely determination.

'Then prove it.'

'Fine. What's the charity?'

He told her and Phoebe jotted down the details. 'What do they do?'

'They help people beat eating disorders.'

She tried and, she suspected, failed to hide her surprise. 'Eating disorders?' What interest could he possibly have in eating disorders?

A muscle twitched in his cheek. 'It's just one of the many charities I'm on the board of.'

'How much do you need to raise?'

Alex named a figure that had Phoebe's head snapping up and her jaw dropping. 'With only twenty-four hours to prepare? That's impossible.'

Alex shrugged. 'If you're as good as Jo seems to think you are, you should have no trouble. If you fail, however, you're fired. Email my secretary for a guest list.' He reached into the breast pocket of his jacket and tossed a card onto her desk.

'This can't be lawful.'

Alex stood up and stared down at her. 'Are you willing to risk it? When did you say Jo's launch was?'

Phoebe's eyes narrowed. How had she ever thought he was gorgeous? The man was ruthless, devious and downright manipulative.

'And if I don't fail?' she said, slowly getting to her feet and clawing back some semblance of control.

'I'll go back to being that silent partner and let you two get on with it.'

Phoebe stuck out her hand and threw him a confident smile. 'In that case, you have a deal.'

CHAPTER FIVE

UGH. WHAT WAS that noise? Phoebe burrowed beneath her duvet and dragged a pillow over her ear while throwing an arm out and taking a swipe in the general direction of her alarm clock. The muffled clatter as it hit the floor and the familiar sound of batteries rolling around the floorboards filtered into her sleep-sodden head. She waited for a second, and then as heavenly silence reigned snuggled down and drifted back into blissful unconsciousness.

Until the shrill ringing started up again.

It hadn't been the alarm clock. Even in her dopey state she could work that one out. She sat up and clamped her hands over her ears but it was no good. Someone was sitting on her doorbell and clearly had little intention of going away.

With a groan, Phoebe untangled herself from the bedclothes and pushed her eye mask onto the top of her head. She staggered to her feet and stumbled to the window. Lifting the sash, she stuck her head out and yelled, 'All right, I'm coming.'

To her intense relief, the infernal racket stopped instantly. She dragged on a silk dressing gown and made her way downstairs, grumbling with every step she took.

Just wait, she thought crossly, marching towards the front door. Whoever was calling at this ungodly hour deserved everything that was coming to them.

'What?' she said heatedly, flinging open the door and getting ready to give the postman a piece of her mind.

But as she glared at the figure standing on her doorstep Phoebe froze. It wasn't the postman. Or the plumber. Or any one of the other possibilities that had vaguely crossed her mind.

It was Alex. Looking good enough to eat in faded jeans and a polo shirt, and a darn sight more together than she was.

'Good morning, Phoebe.'

The bright sunlight burned her retinas and her eyes watered. This really wasn't fair. She lifted her hand to shade her eyes as she stared up at him. 'Uh, morning.'

Alex's leisurely gaze travelled over her and Phoebe bristled at the faint smile that curved his lips. He could laugh all he wanted; he was the one who'd turned up unannounced. If he didn't approve of the state he found her in, he only had himself to blame. 'Can I come in?'

No was the answer on the tip of her tongue. Even though Phoebe suspected she couldn't sink any lower in Alex's estimations, she still had her vanity. She wanted to tell him to go away and come back in an hour. Her current outfit didn't provide much in the way of a defence against a man like him and her hair could probably do with a brush. But as he was already stepping forward there was little she could do to stop him, short of shoving him out and slamming the door behind him, and her head hurt too much for that kind of effort.

'Please do.'

Alex crossed the threshold into the hallway and

Phoebe plastered herself against the wall in an attempt
to prevent any kind of contact. Her hall wasn't small but
he managed to fill it, and even though he hadn't brushed
against her her treacherous body responded as if he had.
A rush of heat shot through her and pooled at the juncture
of her thighs. Beneath the flimsy layers she could feel her
nipples stiffening and with a scowl she wrapped her
dressing gown tightly around her and crossed her arms
over her chest. 'The kitchen's straight on.'

Phoebe followed him into her kitchen, told herself to
ignore the way his T-shirt highlighted the breadth of his
shoulders and the muscles beneath, and set about
making coffee.

'What are you doing here?' she said, sticking her
head in a cupboard and rummaging around for a bag of
beans. 'I didn't expect to see you until this evening.'

'I called, but you didn't answer.'

Phoebe pulled out the beans and a cafetiere and shot
him an accusatory glare. 'I was asleep.'

He leaned against the counter and looked her up and
down again so thoroughly that Phoebe felt as if he'd
stripped her naked. 'So I can see. Out partying?'

She wished. Phoebe's hackles shot up. 'I was up until
five researching your guests,' she said with as much indignation as she could muster. The last couple of hours
of research she'd dedicated to checking him out, but he
didn't need to know that.

'Have you come up with a plan?'

'I have.'

'What is it?'

'Oh, no, I'm not telling you that.'

'Why not?'

'You might sabotage it.'

'I'm not that ruthless.'

'Says the man who'd practically blackmailed me into this weekend.'

'You can back out any time.'

Like that was going to happen. Phoebe's head hurt. It was too early for this. She stifled a yawn.

'What time is it?'

'Ten.'

Hmm. Maybe not that early. But still, five hours of sleep on top of the broken night before was not going to have her firing on all cylinders.

A smile flashed across his face. 'Are you always this irascible?'

'Before coffee and short of sleep, always.' Not to mention being caught by him probably looking like something that had been attacked by a pair of pinking shears.

She didn't need a cup of coffee; she needed a tankerful. Flicking the kettle on she lifted her hand to run it through her hair. Oh, heavens. She still sported the eye mask. How attractive. She yanked it off and dropped it on the table.

'Interesting nightwear.'

Phoebe glanced down at the two scarlet hearts. 'A friend gave it to me on a hen night.'

'It suits you. As does the rest of your outfit.'

His gaze slowly slid down her body and Phoebe felt herself growing as scarlet as the eye mask. She poured the beans into the grinder and switched it on. The noise rattled her brain and Phoebe winced. But at least it might stop her from wondering what he wore in bed. Anything at all would be rather a shame. He'd look amazing sprawled out over her sheets, tanned skin against soft white linen, his eyes darkening with desire…

Phoebe swallowed and gave herself a mental slap. She *really* needed to wake up.

Coffee finally made, Phoebe leaned against the opposite counter and regarded him cautiously. 'So?'

Alex set his cup down and folded his arms over his chest. 'It occurred to me that we hadn't talked about the venue of my party.'

What was he? A mind reader? *'Find out party location'* was the only item left on her 'to do' list. 'I assumed it's somewhere in London. I was going to call you later.'

Alex shook his head in mock despair and gave her a smile that made her stomach lurch. 'Didn't I warn you about the dangers of making assumptions?'

'You did. So enlighten me.' She blew on her coffee and took a fortifying sip. 'Where is it?'

'Ilha das Palmeiras.'

Hmm. Phoebe riffled through all the bars, restaurants and clubs that she knew of, but it didn't ring any bells. 'I might need a bit more to go on than that. Where's Ilha das Palmeiras?'

'It's an island in the mid-Atlantic.'

An island in the mid-Atlantic? Phoebe blinked in confusion. He wanted her to go to an island in the mid-Atlantic? Today? For a party? She needed way more caffeine.

'The current temperature is in the mid twenties,' Alex was saying, 'but it gets chilly at night, so you might want to pack something warm.' He glanced at his watch. 'We need to leave in the next half an hour so I suggest you go and get ready.'

Go and get ready? Phoebe could barely get her head around the implications of what he'd told her. It appeared that not only had he set her a challenge way outside her remit, he also intended her to complete it miles out of her comfort zone.

Devious didn't even begin to describe the workings of his mind, she decided darkly. Machiavelli himself would bow down in awe.

She should have guessed he'd pull a trick like this. It wouldn't have surprised her if he'd deliberately kept the location of the party from her just so he could spring it on her when she was least expecting it. Because in her line of work surprises were never welcome and he must know that.

'Chop chop,' he said mildly, looking at her as if surprised to see her still standing there.

Phoebe huffed, shot him a filthy look and stormed out.

Alex took his coffee into the sitting room and, not for the first time since he'd laid eyes on her scantily clad form, wondered if taking Phoebe with him to the island was really such a wise idea.

The challenge that he'd set her would prove her determination and her commitment and would satisfy his promise to Jo without compromising the vow he'd made to himself in the aftermath of losing everything he'd worked so hard to acquire.

However, the glimpses of long tanned leg that he'd got whenever Phoebe's robe slithered open had tested his control to the limit. That ridiculous eye mask perched on top of her mussed-up hair had got him thinking about blindfolds and silk scarves and hours of lazy sensory exploration and he'd nearly stalked over and pinned her against the counter just to see if she felt as warm and soft as she looked.

There was a thump as something hit the floor above, then a yelp of pain and a string of expletives. Alex snapped back to reality and grinned. Phoebe first thing reminded him of a very grumpy, very put out sprite.

He took a look around. Fat cushions sat at random on the two deep sofas that faced each other either side of a coffee table laden with books. Bright splashes of artwork lined the walls. Piles of magazines were stacked high either side of the fireplace. A book lay open face down on the floor beside the sofa.

The room wasn't messy, but compared to her office it was a tip. If he didn't know otherwise he'd have thought that two very different people occupied each space.

But then nothing about Phoebe was quite as it seemed, he realised, making his way over to the bookcase. Was she the cool, efficient PR executive? The whimpering goddess he'd held in his arms, who'd stared up at him with stars in her eyes and passion infused in her face? Or was she a combination of all of them and more?

'I can't imagine you'll find anything there to interest you.'

Alex swung round and his pulse spiked. Phoebe stood in the doorway, dressed in jeans that hugged her legs and a little cardigan that clung to her curves and pulled tight across her breasts. Dark sunglasses held her hair back from her face.

For a moment Alex couldn't decide which version he preferred. The sleepy, tousled Phoebe who smelled of bed or this sleek, fresh-faced Phoebe who smelled of flowers. And then he realised he was expected to say something. 'That was quick.'

'Yup.' She grinned. 'It's amazing what caffeine can do. And I still have five minutes to spare.'

'I'm impressed. Is that it?' he said, glancing at her suitcase.

'Yes.'

'You travel light.'

'You sound surprised.'

'I am.'

'Not all women carry their entire worldly goods whenever they go anywhere, you know. *My* wardrobe is particularly capsular.'

'Unlike your house. This is very different from your office,' he said, indicating the room with a sweep of his arm.

Phoebe frowned. Generally people didn't see both. She shrugged. 'I don't think clients would be too impressed to see this, do you?'

'Do you care that much what people think?'

She smiled. 'I'm in PR. It kind of goes with the territory.'

'Got your passport?'

'Hmm. Good point.' The phone started ringing and Phoebe walked over to answer it. 'Would you mind? It's in the desk. Top drawer.'

Which reminded her, she needed to get it renewed. And not before time. That photo… The hair. Phoebe shuddered. No one apart from herself and a handful of international immigration officers had ever seen it.

And any second now Alex would be sliding open the drawer, taking it out and flicking through the pages…

'No, wait,' she practically shouted. 'On second thoughts, I'll get it.'

Phoebe dropped the phone and hurled herself at him. Her body slammed into his and Alex let out a gruff oomf at the impact. Her hand covered his, their fingers tangled in the chaos and for a moment she thought the room had started to spin. Showers of sparks shot up her arm. His scent engulfed her and she nearly swooned.

Fighting back a blush, Phoebe tugged her passport out of his grip. 'Sorry about that. Terrible photo.' She peeled herself off him and walked to the door on very wobbly legs. 'We—er—should probably get going.'

CHAPTER SIX

WELL, THAT HAD been gruelling, thought Phoebe, pushing her sunglasses up her nose and taking her first lungfuls of Atlantic air. The flight to the capital had been smooth enough and Alex's skill as a pilot during the short hop to their final destination had been impressive. But having to spend close on to four hours in a confined space with him had been a nightmare.

Once on board his jet, she'd hauled out her laptop with the intention of reading up on her notes, but to her intense irritation her usually excellent powers of concentration had gone on strike. Instead, her body had decided to tune itself to Alex's frequency. Every move he made, every frown, every smile, that flitted across his face registered on her conscience.

But if she'd thought *that* had been torturous it was nothing compared to the torment she'd suffered once they'd transferred to the tin pot of a plane that was to carry them to the party venue.

There'd barely been room to breathe. Alex's shoulder had constantly brushed against hers. His denim-clad thigh had sat inches from her hand and her fingers had itched to reach out and find out if it was as firm and muscled as it looked. And then his voice, coming through her headset, deep and sexy, had reached right down inside her, wrapping itself around her insides and twisting them into knots as he pointed out a pod of whales.

Her body ached from the effort of trying to plaster herself against the side of the plane. Her stomach was still churning. The minute they'd landed she'd been so desperate to get out of the plane she'd nearly garrotted herself.

'Welcome to Ilha das Palmeiras,' Alex said, taking her suitcase and throwing it into the back of the Jeep that was parked at the side of the grass runway.

'It's beautiful.'

'I think so.'

'But humid.' Phoebe could already feel her hair beginning to frizz and rummaged around in her handbag for a hair clip.

'The islanders say if you don't like the weather wait ten minutes.'

Phoebe pinned back her hair and then delved back into her bag for her mobile. Hauling it out, she flipped it open and switched it on. Hmm. She frowned. No signal.

Alex glanced up as she waved it around. 'I wouldn't bother. There's no coverage.'

Oh. 'None at all?' She didn't think she'd ever been anywhere where she hadn't been able to pick up a signal.

'Nope. And there's no landline either.'

'What about the Internet?'

'I'm afraid not.'

There was no need for him to look quite so cheery, thought Phoebe darkly. Her phone was like a third limb. She needed to be available every minute of every day, just in case any nasty little surprises popped up.

But there wasn't much she could do about it now.

With a sigh, Phoebe dropped her phone back into her bag and resigned herself to twenty-four hours of being incommunicado. At least weekends tended to be quiet on the PR front.

The island was smaller than she'd imagined, and far more remote. She'd envisaged a buzzing harbour, bright colours and exotic smells. All that had been true of the island that housed the capital, but Ilha das Palmeiras was quiet and peaceful. After a lifetime of living in London Phoebe had imagined she'd have been more freaked out by the absence of noise, but instead she could already feel herself beginning to unwind.

Palm trees swished in the breeze. The sun warmed her skin. The distant sound of waves crashing onto the shore filled her with a sense of wonderful restfulness.

Maybe after the party, when she'd smashed her target and proved she was more than capable of handling Jo's career, she'd do a spot of sunbathing. Relaxing. God knew how long it had been since she'd had a day off.

'Hop in.'

Phoebe's eyes snapped open. Oh, she had to be careful. If she allowed herself to be lulled into a false sense of tranquillity, if she didn't keep her wits firmly about her, she could find herself struggling to pass Alex's test.

She grappled with the handle of the car door that was welded shut and it dawned on her that she would literally have to 'hop in'. Which she'd never manage with any sort of elegance. Alex had vaulted in, but as she hadn't been inside a gym for years if she tried that she'd land in a heap on the grass. Perhaps if she just perched her bottom on the edge and then levered herself up...

'I would offer you a hand, but I can still recall what happened when I last tried that.'

'Try it again,' she said with uncharacteristic sweetness while batting her eyelashes at him in an exaggerated fashion, 'and I can guarantee you'll get a different response.'

Alex grinned, got out of the car and walked over to her side. 'Turn round.'

Phoebe did and he reached down, put his hands on her waist and lifted her so that she could swing her legs round. He dropped her into the seat and Phoebe untangled her legs and arms. 'Thank you,' she said, determinedly ignoring the tingles zapping around her body and her galloping pulse. 'And since you mention it, thank you for your help with Mark the other night.' Hindsight had made her realise that she might not have been able to manage him on her own, and the fact that she'd never got round to thanking Alex had been niggling away at her ever since.

'You're welcome.' He fired up the engine. 'I probably owe you an apology.'

'Oh?'

'I might have overreacted. Just a bit.'

Phoebe sat back and grinned. 'Accepted. It sounds like you're out of practice.'

'Could be,' he said dryly. 'I don't often have reason to apologise.'

'It must be wonderful being right all the time.'

'Most of the time,' he said with a grin and hit the accelerator.

'So this island must be privately owned,' said Phoebe, clinging onto the top of the windscreen in a futile effort to lessen the jarring on her poor battered body as they bounced over the terrain.

'It is.'

She gave up and went with the motion. 'Who by?'
'Me.'

As she'd suspected. 'Of course. What billionaire would be without one?'

'If I'd wanted a status symbol I'd have bought a playground in the Caribbean.'

Hmm. 'So what is this deserted peaceful island with no interference from the outside world? An escape?'

'Perhaps.'

'From what?' she asked.

'The city.'

She had the impression the island was an escape from more than just the city because she'd found no mention of it in her research. 'How much time do you spend here?'

'Not enough.'

That seemed a shame, she thought, drinking in the spectacular scenery spreading out before her. The shoreline jutted in and out, shaped by millennia of buffeting winds. After the carefully landscaped gardens of the night before last, the rugged beauty of the island took her breath away.

As did Alex's profile. Phoebe took advantage of the fact that he was staring out of the windscreen to study him. Despite the concentration etched on his face, the lines around his mouth and eyes seemed to have softened, as if the serenity of the place had seeped into him too. The wind ruffled his hair and as she ran her gaze over the hint of the bump on his nose it struck her how much Alex suited this landscape.

'When were you here last?'

'About a year ago.'

'Why so long?'

'Busy. Work.'

'What made you buy a remote island in the middle of the Atlantic?'

'It's a remote island in the middle of the Atlantic,' he said dryly. 'I like my space. I value my privacy.'

That figured. Given the press attention he received she guessed he wasn't a great fan of journalists. Or nosy PRs, judging by the brevity of his answers to her questions. Still, she hadn't got where she had by being deflected by evasiveness.

'No man is an island,' she said solemnly.

'Are you romanticising me, Phoebe?'

Heaven forbid. 'Just thought I'd mention it.'

'It's not completely isolated.'

He'd pointed out the other islands in the archipelago as they'd flown over them. 'Who lives on the other ones?'

'No idea.'

'That's not very neighbourly.'

'Owners of remote islands don't tend to be very neighbourly.'

'What happens if you run out of sugar?'

'My housekeeper makes sure I don't.'

He had answers to everything, thought Phoebe as they headed off the rough land and onto a gravel track. He was wasted in venture capital. He should be in PR.

'If you value your privacy so highly, why host a party for a hundred people?'

'No press. Do you have to keep asking questions?'

'Yup. Sorry. It's my job.'

'Perhaps you should be saving your energies for later.'

'I have plenty of energy,' she said with a grin, and realised with surprise that it was true. Despite her lack of sleep, Phoebe felt oddly invigorated. It was probably the sea air. Or the thrill of a challenge. Or perhaps the exhilaration of the Jeep ride.

It had nothing whatsoever to do with having spent the best part of the day with Alex.

A shower of gravel flew up as Alex pulled up outside the house and yanked on the handbrake. The sooner he could get away from Phoebe, the better.

Her incessant questioning was driving him nuts. He didn't want to have to go into detail about when and why he'd bought the island, but any longer and his resistance would crumble under the sheer weight of her persistence.

'Oh, wow.'

Phoebe was standing up and gazing up at his house, an expression of awe on her face. At least she'd stopped with the bloody questions, he thought grimly, jumping out of the Jeep and striding round to her side. 'Give me your hand.'

'This is amazing,' she said, holding her hands out but still staring up at the house. 'Did you build it?'

Alex helped her out of the Jeep, set her on her feet and took their luggage out. 'I designed it. Someone else built it.'

He glanced up. The two-storey glass and steel construction that stood on the edge on the cliff was very different from the glorified shack that had existed when Jo had been recuperating. He'd bought the island primarily for his sister and he'd worked every second to ensure he could do it before she came out of hospital. However it had taken him another couple of years before he'd recouped enough of his previous fortune to build this house.

Memories clamoured at the edges of his brain and Alex ruthlessly pushed them away.

'It's fabulous. The views must be incredible.'

'Go inside and take a look around. You're staying in the capital with the rest of the guests. They're being ferried over and back. But there's a guest wing here you can use in the meantime to get ready or whatever.'

Phoebe's eyebrows shot up. 'If I'm staying with everyone else, why didn't you leave me there when we passed through earlier?'

Good question, he realised with a start. The thought hadn't even occurred to him. But then that was hardly surprising; the moment they'd boarded his plane rational thought had pretty much given up the ghost and a clamouring awareness of the woman with him had taken over. It had left him feeling unusually on edge. 'I thought you might like to check things out in preparation for later.'

She nodded and gave him a smile that made him think of sunshine. 'I would, thanks.'

Alex had had serious doubts about holding a party here. Despite his determination to avoid a repeat of last year, when the event had been held in London and gatecrashed by an extremely creative journalist, the invasion of his privacy and general disruption to what had always been a haven of tranquillity hadn't appealed in the slightest.

However, right now the hive of activity engulfing the house and gardens was as welcome as the unexpected appearance of a life raft in the wake of a shipwreck, and he had no qualms about clinging to it.

He'd go and see that all the arrangements for this evening were in order. Never mind that Maggie was so efficient he didn't need to check anything; if he didn't head off right now he'd be in danger of doing something rash like suggesting a personal guided tour of the bedrooms. He nodded curtly. 'Then I'll leave you to it.'

CHAPTER SEVEN

THIS WAS THE life, Phoebe thought, rolling onto her stomach and feeling the sun hit the backs of her legs. With the gentle sound of the waves lapping at the shore, the breeze rippling through the palm trees, and the softness of the fine sand beneath her towel, she really was in her own little slice of heaven.

Alex's abrupt departure had left her standing there feeling like a spare part and wondering if she'd said something wrong. But she'd pulled herself together, and, after asking around to see if anyone needed any help and being assured that everything was under control, she'd found her way to the guest wing, changed out of her jeans into a skirt and had headed for the relative calm of the beach.

The file with all the details of the guests and the research she'd done lay beneath her cheek. She'd committed pretty much every detail to memory and she'd honed the strategy she'd come up with the night before. If everything went according to plan, within a few hours her position would be safe and she could get back to her life.

In the meantime she intended to take full advantage

of the calm before the storm. She felt herself drifting off to sleep when the sun went behind a cloud. She shivered and reached for her cardigan.

'Working hard?'

Phoebe jolted, manoeuvred herself into a less vulnerable sitting position and squinted up at him. 'I wish you wouldn't keep doing this.'

'What?' Alex said mildly.

'Creeping up on me.'

'Sand's quiet like that.'

So was he, and looming over her like that he was also rather intimidating. The bright sun behind him cast his face in shadow and sunglasses covered his eyes.

He had changed too, ditching the jeans for a pair of khaki shorts. Phoebe couldn't help running her gaze over his legs: tanned and as muscled as she'd imagined. A vision of them entwined with hers charged into her head and her mouth went dry.

This was ridiculous, she scolded herself, swallowing hard. It was just a pair of legs. Everybody had them. Nevertheless it took every drop of strength she possessed to drag her gaze up his body and reach his face. A tiny smile hovered at his mouth and Phoebe instantly realised that he knew she'd been checking him out.

If he mentioned it she'd attribute the pinking of her cheeks to the sun, she decided, pushing herself to her feet and brushing the sand off her skirt. 'What's up?'

'Nothing's up. I'm going for a sail. You're in my way.'

Phoebe glanced round at the acres of sand that surrounded the spot where she'd been lying. 'It's a big beach. Is that yours?' She pointed to the gleaming white yacht moored up against the jetty that stretched out from the beach into the sea.

'It is.'

'Pretty.'

'I think so.'

'What's it called?'

'*She* is called the *Phoenix Three*.'

'Sounds like a pop group. What happened to the *Phoenix One* and *Two*?'

'They sank.'

'And each one rises from the ashes of the previous?'

'Soggy ashes, but something like that.'

'Can I come?' While she'd learned every possible thing she could about his guests, she'd found out precious little about him. How could she do a proper job this evening without knowing as much as possible? Alex had so far proved remarkably adept at dodging her questions. Trapping him on a boat would be ideal.

'Shouldn't you be working?'

'I've done as much as I can from my notes,' she said. 'The rest I'll just have to pick up as I go along.' She smiled winsomely. 'I promise not to get in the way.'

Alex ran his fingers through his hair in a gesture of frustration. He clearly didn't want her on board his yacht. Well, that was tough. She was coming along for the ride whether he liked it or not.

Phoebe glanced down at the cool box he was carrying and decided that she wasn't above a little manipulation herself.

She stared at it longingly. 'Is that lunch?'

'A very late one, yes.'

She widened her eyes and gave him a doleful look. 'You know, I haven't eaten anything all day.'

Alex frowned. 'Didn't you have something up at the house?'

Phoebe bit on her lip and shook her head forlornly. 'I'm ravenous.' She waited and, when Alex didn't look as if he had any intention of taking her hint, she swayed a little. 'Do you realise that if I pass out this evening as a result of lack of sustenance it'll be entirely your fault?'

'How do you figure that?'

'You didn't give me time for breakfast, so if there's enough in there for two…'

'There's plenty.' He set the box on the ground and took the lid off. 'Help yourself.'

Oh. Phoebe peered into the cool box and her mouth watered. Lunch looked and smelled delicious. But however tempting his suggestion was, nibbling on a chicken leg alone on the beach while Alex did whatever he did on boats had not been the plan at all.

'I'd much rather join you,' she said with a little pout.

Alex's jaw tightened but he remained stonily silent.

'Fine,' she said sadly. 'I understand. I just hope your hosting skills improve by tonight.'

Alex let out a resigned sigh. 'OK. That's enough. You can come.'

Phoebe beamed. 'Great.'

Letting Phoebe on board his boat had been such a bad idea, Alex berated himself for the hundredth time.

He should have thrown her a sandwich and left her on the beach. Better still, he should never have disturbed her in the first place. He wasn't sure why he had.

But even though he'd known perfectly well what she'd been up to with those big eyes and the pout it didn't negate the fact that she was right. The catering staff had gone on a break for a couple of hours before gearing up for tonight. The cool box contained enough lunch to feed an army and he was sick of feeling guilty. What else could he have done?

All he'd wanted was a moment's solitude. To feel the wind in his hair, the tiller beneath his hands, and to fill with the sense of peace that sailing always gave him.

But had he found that solitude? That peace? Nope. Because Phoebe was anything but peaceful and he'd been an idiot to think he could get away with ignoring her.

She might not have hit him with a barrage of questions just yet, but her eyes had locked onto him with the focus of a heat-seeking missile the moment they'd cast off and in the past half an hour they hadn't wavered. Even when he had his back to her he could feel her gaze boring into him. Watching him carefully, as if trying to penetrate right through to the centre of him and fathom him out.

His whole body itched and buzzed as if a swarm of bees had taken up residence inside him. The last thing he wanted or needed was fathoming out, he thought grimly, switching off the engine and releasing the main sail. It unfurled and fluttered in the breeze and Alex hauled and winched the ropes until his muscles burned.

For a while the yacht glided smoothly through water, and as Phoebe turned her face to the sun Alex stared at the horizon, let his thoughts lighten and he finally found an edgy sort of peace.

Until Phoebe's stomach rumbled like a crash of thunder and the flicker of guilt he thought he'd managed to extinguish fanned back into life.

'Uh, sorry about that,' she muttered and rubbed her midriff.

'Lunch?'

'I thought you'd never ask.'

If he hadn't had a conscience he wouldn't have.

Because he had no doubt that as soon as they sat down to eat the questions would come. But he couldn't postpone lunch any longer, so he'd answer them as briefly as possible and if she persisted he'd employ any tactic at his disposal to deflect her.

Ignoring an odd sense of impending doom, Alex steered the yacht towards the coast and dropped the anchor as soon as they reached shallow water.

'How did you get to be so good at sailing?' said Phoebe, finishing off the last piece of cold chicken and thinking lunch had never tasted so delicious.

Alex tensed and she wondered exactly why he was so reluctant to talk about himself. 'I used to race.'

'But not any more?' She set the chicken bone on her plate and licked her fingers.

'I gave up a few years ago.' Alex's gaze dipped to her mouth and her lips tingled as if he'd reached out and touched them. A blaze of heat shot through her and she snatched up a napkin.

'Why?' His strength and agility and obvious skill as he leapt around the yacht had had desire and admiration seeping through her in equal measures.

'Better to stop at the top of your game,' he said, his lazy tone completely at odds with the brief awareness that had flared in his eyes.

'Did you ever win?'

'Yes.'

'Big boats or little boats?'

'Both.'

'Solo or in a team?'

'Both.'

Agh. Trying to get information out of Alex was nigh

on impossible. His defences were so high she'd need crampons and breathing equipment to scale them. And as mountaineering had never appealed, Phoebe decided to switch tactic.

'What made you go into venture capital?'

'The bottom line,' he said dryly.

'Is that all?'

'Isn't that enough?'

'Nope.'

Alex shrugged. 'I'm good at it.'

'Very good at it by all accounts.'

He shot her a quizzical glance. 'Have you been checking me out?'

'A little. Of course *I* didn't have time to hire investigators. *I* simply looked you up on the Internet.'

'What did you find?'

'Surprisingly little for someone who has such a high profile.' She'd found heaps of information about his business and his work, but absolutely nothing about his private life. Or Jo, for that matter.

He grinned. 'I'm not that interesting.'

'I don't know about that.' She might as well admit it. She didn't need to know any of this for this evening. She wanted to know about him for herself. Which wasn't all that surprising, she reasoned weakly. She'd always been interested in other people. OK, so she didn't often burn with this degree of curiosity, but then most people weren't so evasive. 'You help people realise their dreams.'

Alex shook his head. 'It's all about maximising return.'

'You helped Jo realise her dream. What return are you expecting from her?'

'Jo's family.'

'What happened to your father?'

'I never knew him. He died the year after I was born.'

'And your stepfather?'

'He married my mother when I was eight. Jo came along two years later. They died six years ago in an avalanche.'

Phoebe's heart squeezed. Her own family might be tricky but she couldn't imagine life without them. 'I'm sorry to hear that.'

Alex shrugged. 'Don't be. They were cross-country skiing at the time and died doing something they loved. I hope you're not going to ask me how I feel about it.'

'I wouldn't dream of it.' He wouldn't tell her even if she had. 'How did Jo take it?'

The change in him was almost palpable. He tensed and his eyes went blank. 'She was devastated,' he said flatly.

Now what was he hiding? she wondered, watching the familiar stony expression set in. Every inch of him was warning her to back off, not to pry any further. Perhaps Jo wasn't the only one who'd been devastated. Perhaps the deaths of his mother and stepfather had had a greater effect on him than he was willing to admit.

Phoebe took a sip of sparkling water and felt the bubbles fizz down her throat. 'You used to have a partner, but now you work alone. Why is that?'

'It's safer.'

'In what way?'

'Other people have a tendency to let you down.'

She could understand that. Letting people down, especially her fabulous overachieving family, was one of the little insecurities that walloped her from time to time.

'Has anyone ever let you down?' she asked.

'Not recently,' he said bleakly.

'What happened?'

'It was so long ago I can barely remember.'

'I don't believe that for a second.'

'Do you ever give up?'

'Nope. I'm kind of tenacious like that. A PR magazine once described me as "subtly yet ruthlessly efficient".'

'I can see why. Although personally I'd call it nosy.' The ghost of a smile hovered at his mouth as he sat back and regarded her thoughtfully.

Phoebe shrugged and grinned. 'It's a useful trait to have in my line of work.' She tilted her head to one side. 'You won't put me off, you know.' His answers were spare and his face gave absolutely nothing away, but she'd get there eventually.

'I know.'

'And I won't fail this evening.'

'Sure?'

Phoebe threw him a confident smile. 'Absolutely. I've done my research and I'm fully prepared. And besides, I'm a Jackson and Jacksons never fail.'

'Never?'

'Never.'

'That sounds like a lot of pressure.'

'Tell me about it.' She rested her chin on her hand and smiled up at him. Maybe if she opened up a bit he would too. 'Actually, I did fail at something once. I swear the look on my father's face was not something I'd ever like to see again. My mother merely shook her head in disappointment and went off to her study.'

Alex visibly relaxed. 'What was it?'

'My fifty metres underwater swimming badge. I was ten.'

His eyebrows shot up.

'I'd had bronchitis. My lungs weren't up to it. But that was no excuse.'

'Of course not,' he said dryly.

'I used to have nightmares about it. I'd be swimming relentlessly up and down a pool with my lungs bursting. I'd pop up to the surface gasping for air, only there'd be a sea of angry faces staring down at me, yelling at me to get back under the water.' That if she didn't try harder she'd fail and she'd be letting them all down.

'And then?'

'Then I'd wake up drenched in sweat with my heart thundering and my head pounding.'

'What did your parents have to say about that?'

'Nothing.' She shrugged. 'They didn't know. I didn't tell them.'

Eventually she'd conquered it. All by herself. Those three months of nightmares had made her stronger. She was sure of it. As had those little blips in her otherwise flawless career.

'That was brave.'

Warmth spread throughout her body. 'Not really.'

'What happened with the swimming test?'

'I had to redo it the next day.'

'Did you pass?'

'Of course. Now I always pass tests,' she said pointedly.

Alex raised an eyebrow.

'I come from a line of overachievers,' she clarified. 'Didn't your…research…throw that up?'

'Some. It turns out I know your brother.'

Oh? 'How?'

'We recently worked together on an IPO.'

That made sense. Dan worked in corporate finance

and made millions on a daily basis. Privately Phoebe thought her brother was heading straight for burnout, but that was his business. She'd tried to question him about it but he'd told her in no uncertain terms to butt out and she'd given up worrying about him.

'Dan is a case in point,' she said and then tilted her head. 'Let me put it like this. In my family Christmas is treated as a business initiative.'

'In what way?'

Right now Alex sounded intrigued. But as soon as she'd explained he'd think her entire family was insane.

'Every September in her role as project manager my mother sends us all an email to establish what we want out of the event. What our *vision* is.'

'Do you have a vision?'

'Well, I don't generally. I'd be happy with a slice of turkey and a cracker. But not the rest of my family. No. We have to decide on our aim. Do we want to push culinary boundaries? Are we going to use the occasion to innovate and experiment, or do we simply want a day of lazy indulgence? That sort of thing.'

Alex was staring at her as if she'd just landed from another planet. 'I know,' she said nodding. 'Nuts. But it gets worse.'

'How could it possibly get worse?'

'Once the key objective has been identified and agreed on, my mother then itemises what exactly is needed to achieve that particular vision and assigns us each roles. Her list can include anything from strategies to prevent my grandmother hitting the gin too early to calculating the number of Brussels sprouts needed. She then informs us of what she expects in terms of performance.'

'Nice relaxing festivities, I imagine.' Amusement glinted in the depths of his eyes.

'Quite. On the actual day she gives us evaluation updates at regular intervals.'

'What happens if something goes wrong?'

Phoebe gave him a look of mock horror. 'Doesn't happen. Contingencies are built in. Should something go awry, and it hasn't since the memorable incident involving my father and a rolling pin ten years ago, we're to simply remind ourselves of the vision. The experience gets absorbed into the following year's strategy.'

'It's probably not a bad way of handling Christmas,' he said dryly.

'Yes, well, next year I'm boycotting it.'

'The family is revolting.'

Phoebe grinned. 'Not at all. My siblings, rather worryingly, embrace the whole thing with gusto, so technically I'm the only one who's revolting.'

'You're not revolting. You're—' Alex broke off, the humour fading from his eyes.

Phoebe's heart skipped a beat at the sudden shift in his demeanour. I'm what? She suddenly longed to know. What am I? Tell me. 'I'm what?' she said and her breath hitched in her throat as she waited for his answer.

Alex blinked and the stormy look in his eyes vanished. 'Going to burn if you're not careful.'

Oh, how annoying was that? He'd been staring at her face as if trying to commit every inch of it to memory, and the way his eyes had darkened as he'd fixed on her mouth had her thinking that concern for her skin had definitely not been uppermost in his mind.

'I'm always careful,' she said loftily.

'So am I,' he muttered, frowning into the distance and

standing up. Alex stretched and then to her consternation reached round the back of his neck and pulled his T-shirt off.

At the expanse of taut brown skin that hit her eyes, Phoebe nearly passed out. Muscles rippled over his abdomen, a smattering of dark hair covered his chest and narrowed down into a fine line that disappeared into the top of his shorts.

She sat on her hands to stop them from darting out and whipping open the button and sliding down his zip. A primitive longing to run her hands over those muscles, to trace the contours of every inch of him, walloped her in the stomach.

'Did I just hear a whimper?' Alex dropped his T-shirt on a deckchair and turned to her, a tiny smile playing at his lips.

'A whimper?' Phoebe snapped her gaze to the horizon and frowned as if in concentration. 'No. I don't think so. I certainly didn't hear a whimper.'

'I could have sworn I did.'

'It must have been the wind.'

'It must.'

'What are you doing?'

'Going for a swim.'

Thank God for that. Who cared if the Atlantic was supposed to be freezing? Or that swimming after eating was generally considered to be a bad thing? If it removed him from sight and out of temptation's way he could swim to the States and she'd cheer him on with every stroke.

'Want to join me?'

Phoebe shuddered at the thought. 'No, thanks. I'll stay here and look after the boat.' And no doubt drive herself mad speculating about what he might have been going to say.

She tried not to stare at his back as he stepped up onto the guardrail, but then figured that, as he couldn't see her, she could sneak a peak. He twisted and stretched, the muscles of his shoulders and back tensing and flexing, and Phoebe had to clamp her mouth shut to stop another whimper escaping.

Alex dived into the clear blue water and as he disappeared beneath the surface Phoebe let out the breath she hadn't realised she'd been holding. It was only when she started putting the remains of lunch back into the cool box that she saw quite how much she was shaking.

By the time Alex stopped his relentless pace, the boat was a speck in the distance, his muscles burned and his lungs stung. The icy water, however, hadn't had the effect he'd hoped.

His body still ached and he felt as tightly wound as one of the yacht's engine coils. Lunch would have had to consist of food that could only really be eaten with fingers, wouldn't it? All that licking and sucking…

And those whimsical little smiles…

If he'd had a superstitious bone in his body he'd have sworn Phoebe had been sent deliberately to torment him. He'd underestimated the madness of letting her on board his boat. The attraction he'd been doing so well at ignoring was getting harder to resist. He wanted her badly. Maybe more than he'd ever wanted anyone before. Which in the general scheme of things was nothing to worry about. Attraction was, after all, a simple question of compatible pheromones.

What worried him considerably more was that he'd

found himself liking her. Admiring her guts, her tenacity and her ability to have survived growing up with so much pressure.

Searing chemistry and liking were a dangerous combination. He'd spent pretty much the whole of the past hour fighting back the increasingly insistent urge to toss aside the table, bundle her into the cabin and get her naked and hot between his sheets.

On more than one occasion during that seemingly interminable lunch he'd been struck by the hammering urge to open up and tell her everything she wanted to know.

The thought doused the heat in his body more effectively than any quantity of ice-cold water. Spilling his guts out to Phoebe, or to anyone for that matter, was never going to happen.

Alex turned round and started ploughing through the water back to the yacht. As soon as he reached it they'd be heading back to the island and the safety of numbers.

His boat definitely wasn't big enough for both of them. He had the uncomfortable suspicion the island wasn't either.

CHAPTER EIGHT

PHOEBE STOOD IN front of the mirror and assessed her reflection with a critical eye. Outwardly she looked exactly as she'd intended. Immaculate, groomed and unflappable. The dress she'd chosen was a reliable favourite, her make-up was flawless and her hair was poker straight.

But her eyes held a worrying sparkle and her cheeks were tinged with pink and inside her stomach churned and her heart raced. Try as she might to persuade herself otherwise, deep down she knew perfectly well it had nothing to do with the thrill of the challenge she was about to face.

Apart from a curt 'it's getting late, we should be heading back', she and Alex hadn't exchanged a word on the journey back to the island, but the care with which they'd kept well out of touching range and had avoided eye contact had spoken volumes. The tension had reached an unbearable level by the time they'd reached the island and neither of them had been able to get off the yacht fast enough.

The minute they'd reached the house Alex had dashed off muttering something about seeing to any

last-minute arrangements. Phoebe had holed up in the
safety of the guest wing where she'd spent so long ana-
lysing the attraction she seemed to have for Alex and
worrying about what might happen if it spiralled out of
control that it had given her quite a fright to realise that
she only had half an hour to get ready.

But now she was. Armour-plated, prepared for battle
and in total command of herself.

It wouldn't get out of control. She simply couldn't
let it.

She glanced out of the window and couldn't help
smiling at the magical scene that spread out below. In the
distance a brightly lit ferry was making its way to the
island. Flaming torches lined the path from the jetty up
the steps to the house and strings of fairy lights looped
from tree to tree. Tables had been set up around the pool
and groaned with food. A string quartet had parked themselves in one corner and were busy tuning up.

Whoever had organised all this had done an amazing
job, thought Phoebe, idly casting her eyes over the
scene. Such a shame that there'd be no press here to
witness the results.

Then her gaze snagged on the man striding across the
terrace and her breath hitched in her throat. Before she
had time to jump back, Alex stopped and turned and
looked straight up at her. Her knees wobbled and she felt
a shiver race down her spine despite the warmth of the
evening air drifting in through the open window.

Alex tilted his head and softly called, 'Show time,'
before swinging round to go down and greet the guests
who were spilling off the ferry and onto the jetty.

Phoebe took a series of deep fortifying breaths and
ordered her stupidly hammering heart to calm down. So

he looked devastating in black tie. Big deal. A lot of men did. Not many, though, had such a debilitating effect on her nervous system.

Phoebe pulled her shoulders back. She really didn't need a palpitating pulse and a frazzled brain right now. If she wanted to achieve anything tonight, she thought, smoothing out the non-existent wrinkles in her glittering dress as she made her way downstairs, she'd better avoid Alex at all costs.

Alex knocked back the rest of his champagne and then ran a finger around the inside of his collar.

What was Phoebe playing at?

The rational side of his brain knew exactly what she was doing. He'd been watching her for the past couple of hours, working her way into circles of guests, smiling, chatting and no doubt persuading her targets to part with vast sums of cash.

He ought to be impressed. Delighted that she was devoting so much effort to his challenge. One of his contemporaries had even made a point of coming up to him and telling him he thought Phoebe was smashing and was tempted to hire her himself. Above all, he ought to be relieved that Phoebe was proving herself to be as committed and capable as she and Jo had claimed.

So why, instead, was he irritated beyond belief? Why had he had to grit his teeth to stop himself snapping at his colleague that Phoebe wasn't for hire? And why the hell couldn't he take his eyes off her?

Yes, she looked beautiful. Her skin glowed in the warm light. Her eyes sparkled and her dress clung to her curves like a second skin.

But that was no reason why every move she made

should burn into his head. Nor why every smile, every laugh, every touch she bestowed on his guests should send white-hot needles shooting through him.

It was driving him demented. The food tasted like sawdust. The champagne burned his throat. He'd lost track of conversations he'd started. Had to have questions repeated. He'd even snapped the stem of a glass, he'd been holding it so tightly. Much more of this and people would begin to speculate about *his* competency.

Alex had had enough. He'd tried his damnedest to convince himself that he wasn't attracted to her but he'd been fooling himself. When she'd sidled past him earlier in that slinky golden dress his brain had imploded, and ever since the principle thought hammering round his head was how quickly he could dispatch his guests and get Phoebe on her own.

It would help if she hadn't spent the entire night avoiding him, he thought grimly. Everyone else had managed to come up and at the very least compliment him on the evening. Yet all Phoebe had managed to do was maintain her distance. Was it a coincidence that hordes of people had kept them separate throughout the night? He thought not.

'So who is she?'

At the curiosity-laden voice of the woman threading her arm though his, Alex yanked himself out of his thoughts and glanced down. His eyes narrowed at the knowing little smile on Maggie's face and he forced himself to relax.

'Who is who?' he drawled as if he didn't have the faintest idea who Maggie was talking about.

'The brunette you can't take your eyes off.'

Maggie might have known him a long time but that

didn't mean he had any intention of telling her anything. He stiffened. 'She's business.'

'It's funny,' Maggie said with a casualness that didn't deceive him for a second, 'but no business I've ever been involved in has generated the kind of scorching looks you two have been exchanging all evening. I must be doing something wrong.'

'Your business is thriving.'

'Yes, but it would be so much more fun if Jim and I smouldered at each other like that.'

His gaze swung back to Phoebe and his jaw tightened as he watched one of his friends drop a kiss on her cheek. His hands balled into fists. 'Believe me, it's no fun.' At least not yet. Alex's pulse hammered. There was only one way to find out if she was as at the mercy of this attraction as he was.

'Hmm, perhaps not,' Maggie said, glancing down at his white knuckles and easing her arm out of his. 'Is she coming back on the boat with us?'

To end up in the arms of one of the many men she'd been flirting with all night? Not a chance. 'No,' he said grimly, 'she isn't.'

Oh, God, Alex was coming over.

Phoebe glanced round to try and find someone to latch onto and engage in intense conversation but the crowd of people she'd been using as a shield was thinning out and for the first time in the entire evening she was alone.

She ought to be dashing inside and running up the stairs. Chucking her things into her bag and joining the others and getting off this island as soon as possible.

Because she'd done what she'd set out to achieve.

She'd more than completed Alex's challenge, and, assuming he stuck to his word, she'd secured Jo's and her own future, despite every second of the evening being torture. She had no further reason to stay.

So why wasn't she making a run for it? Why wasn't she seeking out the guest who'd offered her a lift on his private jet and looking forward to being back in London before sunrise? Why did her feet remain rooted to the ground?

Phoebe's heart began to gallop as Alex closed the distance between them. He could have been born to wear black tie. He looked incredible. Dark and brooding and devastatingly handsome. He looked even better without the willowy blonde draped all over him, she thought tartly.

As he strode towards her, grim determination etched into his features, and a wild look in his eye, he pulled off his tie and snapped open the top button of his shirt, and Phoebe's head spun.

An image of her undoing the rest of those buttons and tugging his clothes off him flew into her head and she nearly buckled beneath the force of the desire that whipped though her.

She swallowed hard and tried to ignore it, but it was no use. She couldn't deny it any longer. She wanted Alex. She wanted him so badly that all he'd have to do was switch on the charm and the last vestiges of her resistance would crumble.

Her fingers itched to touch him. Her mouth tingled with the need to feel his lips moving over hers. She didn't care any more. She might have successfully managed to avoid him, but his eyes had been on her all night, burning through the flimsy fabric of her dress and tangling up her insides. When their gazes had locked the hungry fire in his eyes had fanned the flames of desire that swept along her veins and all she wanted now was to assuage this deep craving that consumed her.

Alex stopped in front of her and Phoebe's breath caught.

'You look as if you've been enjoying yourself.'

Enjoying herself wouldn't be quite how she'd describe the torment of trying to concentrate while battling the threat that the constant awareness of where Alex was and who he was with posed to her composure. 'I have,' she answered, inwardly amazed at how steady her voice sounded when inside she was a quivering mass of need. 'It's been a lovely party. Beautifully done.'

He shoved his hands in his pockets and his eyes glittered down at her. 'And my challenge?'

'Completed and detailed here.' She held up a little notebook. 'Impressed?'

A muscle pounded in his jaw. 'I'd be a lot more impressed if you'd managed it without all the flirting.'

What? For a moment Phoebe could do nothing more than gape at him. Then she snapped her mouth shut and told herself to hang on before leaping to the wrong conclusion. 'If you'd wanted to draw up conditions about how I raised the money,' she said with a calmness she really didn't feel, 'you should have mentioned them before.'

'I would have had I thought you'd resort to such obvious measures.'

That was it. The disdain in his voice tipped her over and a sudden explosion of anger erupted inside her. She'd done everything he'd demanded of her and for him to then turn round and accuse her of flirting... A swirling mass of incandescence and hurt and something strangely like disappointment boiled in her veins. How could he even *think* that was what she'd been doing? Hadn't he learnt *anything* about her?

'I wasn't flirting,' she said icily. 'It's called taking an interest. Conversation. The exchange of information. Not that you'd know much about that.'

Alex let out a humourless laugh. 'So the people you set your sights on just doled out the cash in a sudden fit of generosity?'

His voice dripped with sarcasm and Phoebe just wanted to get as far away from him as possible. 'No, they didn't. They offered things. Jewellery. Holidays. Wine.'

'I bet they did. To you?'

'No, of course, not to me,' she snapped witheringly. 'For the auction you're going to have at your charity event. So good luck with that.'

Alex went very still. Good. She hoped he froze to the spot. She slapped her notebook against his chest barely noticing it fall to the ground. She didn't care if she never saw him again, the arrogant, patronising jerk.

She turned on her heel but then stopped suddenly and whipped back. 'And just for the record, those donations? Three quarters of them came from women.'

Oh, *hell*.

Alex watched Phoebe storm off into the house and called himself every name under the sun. He wanted to hit something. Hard. Preferably himself.

He bent down to pick up the notebook and flicked through it as he straightened. Page after page of handwriting detailed each donation, the estimated value and the contact details of the donor.

He totted up the total. Phoebe hadn't just completed

his challenge. She'd raised double the original target. Dammit, he *was* impressed. So what on earth had prompted him to attack her like that?

Alex thrust the notebook into his pocket and strode after her. He took the stairs two at a time and found her in the guest wing, whirling round the room like a dervish, flinging things into her bag and muttering furiously under her breath.

He stopped in the doorway. 'Phoebe.'

Phoebe spun round. Her cheeks were red and her chest was heaving, but she didn't stop moving. 'Go away.'

Alex had no intention of going anywhere. The need to finish what had started beneath the pergola clawed at his stomach. 'I'm sorry,' he said. 'I shouldn't have implied that you'd sell yourself to bring in business. It was a careless thing to say and totally unfounded.'

'No,' she said. 'You shouldn't. So why did you?'

He ran his hands through his hair. 'I was angry.'

'About what?

'That dress would tempt a saint.'

That stopped her in her tracks. She stuck her hands on her hips and glared at him. 'So now it's *my* fault?'

He frowned. 'Were you aware of the looks you were attracting?'

'The only looks I noticed were the filthy ones you kept flinging in my direction.'

'You smiled at and talked to everyone yet you avoided me. All night,' he ground out.

Phoebe's lip curled. 'You sound jealous.'

Alex blinked and felt faintly stunned. He'd never experienced jealousy, but it certainly explained a lot. 'You're right. I was.'

Her eyes flashed. 'Again, not my fault.'

'Why were you avoiding me?'

'I wasn't,' she snapped, but her gaze slid away and he knew she'd been doing exactly that. 'I had little time and a long list of people to talk to. I couldn't afford to waste a second.'

'Is that the only reason?'

'What other reason would there be?'

'Perhaps I distract you.'

'Don't flatter yourself.' She swivelled round and stuffed the rest of her things into her bag.

'Where are you going?'

'To catch the boat.'

'Don't.'

'What?'

'Stay here,' he said. 'With me.'

Phoebe froze. 'Why would I want to do an insane thing like that?'

Alex took a deep breath and started towards her. 'Because I think you want me as much as I want you. If I'm right then it's tearing you up as much as it's tearing me up. I don't know about you, but I can't take it much longer.'

For several long seconds absolute silence hit the room and then the air began to vibrate with electricity. Phoebe stared at him, her eyes darkening and her breathing quickening. For a moment Alex thought she was going to hurl herself into his arms and adrenalin and lust surged through him.

But her face suddenly went blank and the shock of it nearly winded him. 'If you're after a bit of attention I suggest you cuddle up to the blonde,' she said acidly.

Bewilderment sliced through the heavy beat of desire. 'What blonde?'

'The one surgically attached to your arm.'

The penny dropped and Alex felt like punching the air with relief. Phoebe was jealous, which meant he'd been right. She did want him. 'You mean Maggie?'

Phoebe frowned. '*That* was Maggie? Your house-keeper, Maggie?'

'She's more than just a housekeeper. She organised this evening. She used to plan events in London.'

'Good for her,' she said tartly.

'We go back a long way. I was in a solo race once and hit a storm. My mast broke and I capsized just off the coast. She picked up my distress signal and towed me in.'

'Kind of her.'

'I thought so, especially since I'd broken a leg, an arm and a couple of ribs.' If he'd blinked he'd have missed the wince that flashed across her features. 'We've been friends ever since.'

Phoebe stuck her chin up. 'I really don't know why you're telling me all this.'

'Would it interest you to know that she and Jim, her husband, run a chandler's over in the capital?'

Something flickered in the depths of her eyes. 'Not in the slightest.'

'Liar,' he said softly and pulled her into his arms.

CHAPTER NINE

THE MINUTE HE reached for her, Phoebe was lost. What was left of her resistance fled. Crushing disappointment and excoriating anger switched to thumping relief and scorching desire. As Alex wrapped her tightly in his embrace Phoebe flung her arms around his neck. His mouth met hers. Teeth clashed and tongues duelled and as they kissed the heat that spun through her made her melt against him.

As the kiss softened and deepened Phoebe clutched at Alex's jacket, desperate to be able to slide her hands beneath his shirt and feel the warm skin of his back.

Her breasts swelled, nipples tightening and pushing painfully against the bodice of her dress. She could feel the thick, hard length of his erection pulsing against her stomach and she filled with a desperate ache to have him filling her, pounding into her, sending her into oblivion.

While his mouth continued to devour her, Alex's hands slid down her back, over the curve of her bottom, and pulled her tight against him and Phoebe moaned. She'd never felt anything like this before. This primitive craving. This total abandonment. The throbbing conviction that if she didn't have him deep inside her she'd die.

As their kisses grew more ravenous Alex slid the zip of her dress down and it fell in a pool of shimmering silk at her feet. Phoebe shoved his jacket off and tugged at his shirt, dismayed by the number of studs there were to undo. But Alex pulled it over his head, and got rid of the rest of his clothes and hers, and then they were tumbling onto the bed.

Their hands roamed over each other, stroking and rubbing and caressing slick hot skin until they were both shaking with need.

'Please tell me you have a condom somewhere,' Alex groaned against her mouth.

Phoebe froze and felt like wailing. 'Of course I don't have a condom with me. I didn't come here for sex.'

He pulled back and stared down at her, his eyes blazing with frustration. 'Damn. Neither did I.'

The ferocity of the disappointment that thundered through her took her breath away. But then Alex gave her a wicked smile that had all sorts of delicious thoughts running through her head. 'But that doesn't mean we can't still have a heck of a lot of fun.' He began kissing his way down her neck.

Phoebe fell back and let herself drown in the sensations pulsating through her and tried to ignore her disappointment. Part of her wished she were irresponsible enough to tell Alex she didn't care about protection. But then look what had happened as a result of exactly that to the friend whose hen night she'd been to. Furious parents and a shotgun wedding. Not her idea of fun. Although...

'Stop. Wait.'

Alex lifted his head and stared at her in disbelief. 'Are you serious?'

'I do have condoms. A pack of six.' Handed out by her friend with the solemn warning to always take care.

'Where?' he said hoarsely.

'My suitcase. Front pocket.'

Alex rolled off her and was back within seconds ripping away the plastic with his teeth and emptying the box onto the bedside table.

'Always prepared?' he said.

'A hen weekend,' she said, her voice suddenly husky.

'Sounds like an interesting weekend.'

'We learned to pole dance. I can show you later if you—'

Phoebe didn't get to finish her sentence. Alex came down on top of her and crashed his mouth down on hers. Desire slammed straight into her as his lips and tongue embarked on a devastating assault that ravaged her senses. Her pulse galloped. Her legs trembled. She kissed him back greedily, seeking more of him and getting it as the kiss deepened. Her body softened. Her fingers twisted in his hair and she pressed herself even closer to him.

The heat of his mouth, the hardness of his body threatened to send her hurtling out of control. Phoebe's head began to spin with the deep yearning to have him inside her. She itched and throbbed and ached. His erection pressed against her and her thighs fell apart.

Her chest was heaving with the effort of struggling to breathe. 'Now,' she whispered, half crazed with need, her fingers digging into his shoulders.

It must have been the desperate pleading in her voice that broke the grip on his control. Because a second later Alex had rolled the condom on, and she could feel the tip of his penis nudging at her entrance and let out a soft low moan.

'You're very beautiful,' he murmured, bending his head and kissing her slowly and thoroughly.

Delight flooded through her and, just when she thought she was about to pass out from the anticipation, Alex thrust into her. Her inner muscles instantly clamped round him as if never wanting to let him go.

The tightness was back in the pit of her stomach, drawing all her attention to it, sucking her into a black hole of aching need. Phoebe wrenched her mouth from his and panted. Alex groaned and went still, as if the merest movement would send him over the edge.

He felt so incredibly good, deep inside her. Better than anything she could have possibly imagined. Her pulse started to race, her breathing shallowed and she couldn't prevent her hips from arching up. Her hands found their way to his back, and she pressed and traced his muscles, biting on her lip to stop herself from crying out at the incredible sensations that rolled through her, stronger and wilder than anything she'd ever felt before.

Phoebe's insides started to unravel and she felt the beginnings of an earth-shattering climax roll towards her.

And then it was as if Alex lost the thread on his control. He began to move, pulling out of her and then driving in deeper and harder and faster until they were both spiralling towards a peak that they hit at the same time. With a tiny cry, Phoebe broke apart and heard Alex's hoarse groan as he collapsed on top of her.

Long seconds passed during which the only sounds she could hear were her tiny gasps for breath and the thundering of her heart.

'I can't believe that just happened,' she said shakily.

Alex gently pulled away from her and rolled onto his back. 'Can't you? I can't believe it didn't happen before.'

'If I'd known it was going to be like that, I'd have suggested it earlier.'

'No, you wouldn't. Any more than I would have.'

'Well, I'm glad I've finally found out what the fuss is about,' she said feeling a drowsy smile spread across her face.

'What?'

Phoebe stilled. Oh, heavens, had she actually said that out loud? 'Er—nothing.'

Alex propped himself up on his elbow and frowned down at her. 'Please don't tell me you were a virgin.'

If only it were that simple. 'Oh, no,' she said, aiming for breezy nonchalance and failing dismally. 'I've had sex. Loads of it. Well, not that much,' she amended, seeing his raised eyebrow. And probably not nearly as much as he had, judging by his skill. 'But I've never…' Her gaze slid over his shoulder and focused on the white gauzy curtain fluttering in the breeze. She could scarcely believe she was about to tell him this. 'You know…enjoyed it that much.'

'You've never had an orgasm?' Alex sounded stunned.

'No. Well, I mean, not really.'

'What on earth do you mean? Either you have or you haven't.'

Phoebe felt her cheeks flame. 'I've always managed perfectly well on my own, but never, er, with anyone else.'

'Much more fun with someone else, don't you think?' he said, smiling down at her.

'Heaps.' She grinned. 'You look pleased with yourself.'

'I gave you your first orgasm. What man wouldn't be pleased about that?'

'And, hallelujah, it proves I'm not frigid after all.'

'Why would you think you're frigid?'

Phoebe's grin faded and she shrugged as if it hadn't bothered her in the slightest. 'I've been told so. On various occasions.'

Alex curled a lock of hair around his finger and tugged her head forwards for a scorching kiss. 'I think we've dispelled that myth,' he said when he eventually came up for air.

'If you get told something often enough you end up believing it. So I decided it probably wasn't worth the bother. You know how I feel about failure. Jacksons tend to avoid things they're not particularly good at.'

'It's not your failure. It's the failure of the men you've slept with.'

Phoebe grinned and glanced up at him. 'I like that.' She ran a finger over his scar and he flinched. 'How did you get this?'

'The same way I got this,' he said, tapping the slight bump on his nose.

'Sailing?'

'A fight.'

Phoebe's eyebrows shot up. 'About what?'

Alex lay back and stared up at the ceiling. 'It was so long ago I can't remember.'

'Was it over a woman?'

'I think it may well have been.'

'Did you win?'

'Yes.'

Phoebe smiled. Of course he won. 'Would you like to see mine?'

Alex rolled onto his side and looked down at her. 'You have a scar?'

'I do.'

'What from?'

'I once fell out of a tree.'

'What were you doing up a tree?'

'Rescuing a scarf.'

His brows snapped together. 'Are you mad?'

'The most beautiful cashmere scarf. I was sixteen.'

'You fell from a tree when you were sixteen and all you ended up with was a scar? You were lucky not to have been killed.'

'So they told me. I was a clumsy teenager.'

'Where is it?'

'Hanging up in my wardrobe at home, I think.'

'Very funny. I was talking about the scar.'

'Didn't you see it earlier?'

Alex shook his head. 'My mind must have been on other things.'

'Well,' she said, batting her eyelashes and throwing him a sultry smile, 'why don't you try looking for it?'

CHAPTER TEN

THE SUNLIGHT FILTERING through the curtains gradually roused Phoebe from her sleep. For a split second she couldn't work out where she was, but as the events of the night before rolled through her head she grinned and stretched and felt like purring.

She shifted onto her side and opened one eye to double check she hadn't been dreaming. At the empty space beside her, Phoebe's heart plummeted. Then she saw the indent on the pillow and felt the lingering heat of Alex's body on the sheet and her spirits soared.

Her body ached deliciously. Alex had seemed set on making up for all those years of mediocre sex and she'd decided it would be churlish to stop him. The argument about who suffered the least from jealousy had been resolved in a highly satisfactory manner.

But as the sounds of people clearing up outside dragged her into the day the implications of what she'd done began to set in and the doubts she'd managed to keep at bay throughout the long hot night crowded at the edges of her brain.

However inevitable and incredible the night had been, one thing was undeniable. She'd gone to bed with her client's brother. The man who still had the power to ruin her, despite her success at the party.

What would happen now?

A cold film of sweat broke out all over her skin as her mind raced through a variety of different scenarios, none of which allayed her worries in the slightest.

Her thoughts were still a mess when she heard footsteps on the landing. Phoebe pulled the sheet up to her chin as if it might provide some sort of defence against what he might have to say about her conduct.

Alex appeared at the doorway looking all gorgeous and rumpled, carrying two cups of coffee and wearing nothing but jeans and, despite her concerns, desire surged through her.

'Good morning,' he said, walking over to the bed where Phoebe lay quivering beneath the sheets. He didn't look as if he had a problem with her behaviour last night, she thought as he set the cups down on the bedside table. But who knew? He could be lulling her into a false sense of security. Getting her all languid and pliable before, bam, he hit her with the news that he'd decided to install his own team after all.

His own team, who probably wouldn't jump into bed with him at the first available opportunity.

He sat down and planted his hands either side of her. Phoebe felt like groaning and burying her face in the pillow. 'Uh, morning.'

Alex leaned down and kissed her. He'd brushed his teeth. That really wasn't fair.

'Phoebe?' he said, pulling back and looking down at her with concern.

'Uh-huh.'

'What's the matter?'

'Nothing.'

He frowned. 'Do you regret last night?'

'No. Yes. Maybe.' Her gaze slid over his shoulder and she bit on her lip. 'Do you?'

'Not at all.'

'Oh,' she said, slightly disconcerted by the gleam in his eye. 'Good.'

'So what is it?'

'I was just wondering where I stand with regard to the job.'

He visibly relaxed. 'Is that all?'

'All?' She glared at him. 'Don't you realise how important it is to me?'

'I have some idea.'

'I'd do pretty much anything to hang onto it.'

'Anything?' He arched an eyebrow.

Phoebe blushed. 'Well, not anything exactly.' She paused. 'I hope you don't think I went to bed with you to secure it or something.'

'I don't think that. At least I didn't.' He frowned slightly. '*Did* you go to bed with me to secure it?'

'Of course I didn't,' she said heatedly. 'I went to bed with you because it had got to the stage when I couldn't not. You were right. This…' How could she begin to describe it?

'Chemistry.'

'Yes, chemistry…has been tearing me apart.'

Alex grinned. 'Well, I'm glad that's cleared up.'

'It's not cleared up.'

Alex ran a hand through his hair. 'Is this conversation ever going to make sense?'

'Agh.' She batted him on the arm. 'Just tell me. Do I or do I not have the job?'

'You do.'

Phoebe flopped back onto the pillows as relief flooded through her. Then a thought struck her and she froze. 'Not because of last night?'

'Of course because of last night, but not the part you're thinking of. I think the strategy you came up with to raise the money was inspired and executed brilliantly.'

Phoebe beamed. Thank heavens for that. 'So just to make sure I've got this right, I continue working with Jo and you go back to being a silent partner?'

Alex grimaced as if the thought of taking a step back was hard to swallow. 'Something like that.'

'Can I have it in writing?'

'Don't push your luck.'

Phoebe grinned and levered herself upright to plant a kiss on his mouth. 'The thought of relinquishing control drives you nuts, doesn't it?'

He shot her a thoughtful glance. 'Not as much as I anticipated. And I dare say I'll get used to it.'

Then he looked over her hair and a faint smile hovered at his mouth. 'I like this.'

Phoebe's heart skipped a beat. She dreaded to think what sort of state her hair was in. In the middle of the night Alex had carried her into the shower and had made love to her so thoroughly she hadn't given it a moment's thought. Now, though, she wished she'd at least run a brush through it while it had still been wet. 'Don't mock. It's a sore point.'

'I'm not mocking,' he said mildly, shooting her a quick smouldering smile. 'It suits you.'

'Huh?'

'It goes with the rest of you.'

Phoebe frowned. 'Springy?'

'Curvy.'

Curvy? What woman wanted to be described as curvy? 'I'm not sure I like curvy.'

'I do,' said Alex, running a hand up her body and cupping her breast.

Phoebe bit on her lip to stop herself from moaning and tried to concentrate. 'I always wanted to be a sleek blonde.'

To her great disappointment Alex removed his hand and tilted his head. She should have kept quiet and moaned after all. 'Why?'

'My sister is a sleek blonde. I peroxided my hair once but it went green, so I decided to stick to being a sleek brunette instead.'

'I prefer brunettes. And I prefer ruffled.'

Ruffled was good. Ruffled sounded seductive in a sort of louche sex-kitten kind of way. 'You do?'

Alex's eyes gleamed. 'Uh-huh. And right now, I don't think you're ruffled enough.'

'So what are you going to do about it?'

'Hmm, let me see… Where shall I start?' He ran his eyes over her as if assessing every inch of skin. 'How about here?' He bent his head and dropped a kiss at the base of her neck. Phoebe shivered. 'No?' He hooked a finger over the top of the sheet and pulled it down. 'All right, how about here?' He ran a trail of kisses down the slope of her breast and flicked his tongue over her nipple. Phoebe's back arched and she gasped.

'Feeling ruffled yet?' He lifted his head and looked into her eyes. It felt as if he could see right into her soul and Phoebe had the sudden premonition that Alex could turn out to be very bad for her indeed.

'Getting there,' she said huskily.

The sound of a phone ringing somewhere downstairs

jolted her out of the haze of desire. 'I thought you didn't have a phone.'

'There's a satellite phone,' he murmured against her skin.

'Shouldn't you go and answer it?'

'Too late.'

The ringing stopped as the answer machine kicked in.

Phoebe grinned and stretched back. 'Don't you just love civilisation?'

'Where would we be without it?'

'The Stone Age?' she said softly. 'In fact I can just see you in a loin cloth, hunting and gathering.'

Alex lifted his head and his eyes gleamed. 'I can see you lying on the floor of my cave waiting to be ravished on my return.'

'I wouldn't,' said Phoebe indignantly, thinking how wonderfully wanton that sounded. 'I'd be decorating. Doing something creative with shells. Drawing on the walls. Or alternatively I'd be sitting with the other cave-women and listening to how they sent their men out for some leaves and roots for supper and they came back with a woolly mammoth.'

Alex laughed and the sound of it rumbled right through her making every nerve ending tingle.

'Besides, it would be *our* cave, not just yours.'

Alex pulled back a little and Phoebe wondered what she'd said. 'Alex?'

'Phoebe.' The cool tone of his voice sent an involuntary shiver down her spine. 'Before we go any further, you should know I'm not looking for a cave with anyone.'

No. In the past five years he hadn't been photographed with the same woman twice. 'You're the one who mentioned me lying in your cave.'

'Yes, but I didn't have you decorating.'

If he hadn't been lying half on top of her, she'd have kicked herself. 'My mistake. I don't really like decorating anyway. The decorative arts were shunned in the Jackson household in favour of academia, so I'd probably have to get someone in.'

He frowned. 'You're missing my point.'

'No, I'm not. I understand perfectly well what you mean. You needn't worry. I'm not going to get all clingy and needy. The last thing I need at this stage in my career is anything serious or heavy.' She shot him a smouldering smile. 'But the hot sex is kind of nice.'

'Nice?' he murmured. 'I must be out of practice.'

Yeah right. 'I guess you have it a lot,' she said lightly. 'What with being an international playboy and things.'

'Not as often as you might imagine. And don't tell anyone, but I'm not much of a playboy either.'

A kick of something resembling delirious relief punched her in the stomach and alarm bells rang in her ears. Oh, if she wasn't careful she could find herself careering down such a slippery slope.

'Ever been in love?'

'Phoebe…'

'OK, OK,' she said, grinning. Neither had she, and frankly the idea of being at the mercy of rampaging emotions made her feel sick just thinking about it. 'So all those photos… all that arm candy…?'

'Just arm candy.' He paused and lifted an eyebrow. 'Is there anything else you'd like to know?'

Everything, she thought, feeling unaccountably pleased at his answer. She wanted to know everything about him. But not right now… 'About that hot sex,' she said, throwing him a coquettish smile. 'Any chance of some more?'

Alex listened to the soft sound of Phoebe's breathing as she dozed. Her head lay on his chest, and her arm was flung across his stomach. Sleep, however, eluded him completely. He'd never felt more awake or more alert.

The way Phoebe had responded to him over and over again astounded him. Once she'd had her eyes opened, she'd been insatiable. And he'd been more than willing to help her make up for lost time. But if he wasn't careful this could get way out of hand. By now, he'd have expected the itch to have gone away. That after the night they'd just had, desire would have faded. But it hadn't. Quite the opposite. Even now, he could feel himself stirring again.

What was it about her? He stared down at Phoebe's face and felt a weight shift in his chest. Something bordering on panic gripped his insides and he suddenly felt an odd desperation to escape. He gently lifted her arm and eased himself from beneath her.

Phoebe stirred and made a little sound of protest. 'Where are you going?' she said sleepily.

'To see who that was on the phone. Don't go anywhere.'

Oh, good Lord. Phoebe stood in the bathroom and stared at her reflection in absolute horror.

When Alex had said he liked her hair like this he had to be lying. Frizzy didn't even begin to describe the mess. Her hair stuck out at bizarre angles, as a result of her going to sleep with it wet and Alex's fingers tangling through it all night. Her poor overworked straighteners would never be able to tame this. She needed an industrial tool kit, the likes of which she'd only ever found in a handful of London salons. She'd head to the nearest one just as soon as they landed back on British soil.

And then what? Would Alex suggest dinner? Should she suggest a drink? Nervous excitement fizzled around her stomach. Or might that be too clingy for something which was only about hot sex? She was sailing into uncharted territory here, she realised, frowning at her reflection. She'd better figure out the rules. Maybe she'd ask Alex. He was bound to have a whole string of them.

'Phoebe.'

The sound of his voice jerked her out of her thoughts. She couldn't let him see her like this. Horizontal, with her hair spread out over a pillow or his chest was one thing. Vertical was quite another.

'Just a minute.'

He flung the bathroom door open and as she swung round every niggle about her hair and rules flew from her head. Alex looked absolutely terrible. His face was white. His eyes were stormy grey and filled with concern.

Phoebe's heart lurched. 'What's happened?'

'We need to leave.'

'Now?'

'Immediately.'

'Why?'

'That was Jo on the phone.'

Fear gripped her stomach and she clutched at the basin. 'Is she all right?'

'Physically she's fine. Mentally I'm not sure. The press have got hold of a story about her.'

Oh, no. Phoebe went very still. 'What about?'

'How much has she told you about her life before design college?'

'Not a lot. I guess I'd imagined she'd been at school.'

'She was. While she was there she became anorexic and ended up in a psychiatric hospital.'

Her stomach churned. 'How long for?'

'A year.'

God, how awful. Phoebe could barely begin to imagine what Jo must have gone through. 'And that's the story?'

'In a nutshell.'

So much for her rash assumption that weekends in PR were quiet. She should never have tempted fate like that. Feeling as if the walls were closing in on her Phoebe dragged in a shaky breath. 'Can I use the phone? I'd like to check my messages.'

Alex nodded briefly. 'It's in the study. As soon as you're ready we'll leave.'

Thirty-five missed calls.

Fifteen messages before the time had run out.

Messages from Jo. Growing increasingly frantic. From the fashion house wondering what the hell was going on. From journalists asking for comments and verification of the facts. From potential clients cancelling meetings and postponing lunches.

All wanting to know where Phoebe was and why she wasn't answering her phone.

As realisation dawned her heart began to thud and panic clawed at her stomach. Her palms went damp and a ball of dread lodged in her throat. A bolt of sheer terror gripped her insides and squeezed. Her vision went fuzzy as a wave of nausea reared up from her stomach to her throat. Blindly Phoebe stumbled to the window, threw it open and sucked in great gulps of air.

Everything she'd ever worked for, everything Jo had

ever worked for, hung in the balance. She knew the field she worked in well. If she was there, on the scene, she'd be able to reassure people that she was in full control and handling the crisis. If she was there she'd be able to divert disaster.

Instead where was she? Miles away. And what had she been doing while Jo was falling to pieces and her whole life was threatening to implode? Laughing and talking and exploring the new-found delights of sexual ecstasy with Alex.

Phoebe felt like banging her head against the desk as a tidal wave of guilt flooded through her. She'd allowed herself to get distracted and taken her eye off the ball. How could she have been so stupid?

And the principle thought running round and round her head on the tense and fraught journey back to London was that it had happened again.

Phoebe read the story for the third time, then closed the newspaper and tried to rally her spirits, but it was as bad as she'd imagined.

According to the report, Jo had once had a boyfriend who'd bullied her, nagged her about her weight and introduced her to diet pills, which had led to addiction, extreme anorexia and the subsequent hospitalisation.

She could scarcely believe that the girl described in the article and the girl sitting next to her on the sofa were one and the same.

'Is all of this true?' Phoebe said, more to break the taut silence than out of any necessity to know the answer. Whether it was true or not, the damage had already been done, as the messages on her mobile and in her inbox testified.

'Pretty much.' Jo sniffed. Her eyes were red and puffy, but she was holding up remarkably well given the circumstances.

'Is there any more?'

'No.'

Thank goodness for that. 'Why didn't I know about this?'

'No one does,' said Alex flatly.

Phoebe glanced over at him and steeled herself against the effect Alex had on her brain. She really needed a clear head at the moment. 'Well, someone clearly does... A source close to Ms Douglas...' She turned to Jo. 'Can you think of anyone that might be? Someone who worked at the hospital perhaps?'

Jo sighed. 'I suspect it might have been Mark.'

A stunned hush fell over the room.

'Mark?' Alex's voice sliced through the silence like a whip.

Jo slumped back against her worktable. 'I might have mentioned that I once had problems with my weight and I haven't been able to get hold of him since the party.'

Phoebe's brain raced. 'If he was broke, then he may well have sold what he knew to the papers. Once a journalist gets the sniff of a story it usually doesn't take much digging to uncover the rest.'

The memory of Mark's drunken threats flashed into her head and she cast a quick glance at Alex. The haggard look on his face told her that he'd come to a similar conclusion.

'I'm sorry I wasn't here when you called.'

Jo gave her a wan smile. 'It doesn't matter. You're here now. But where were you? I've never not been able to get hold of you before.'

Jo sounded more curious than accusatory, but that didn't stop guilt washing over her. 'I was away,' said Phoebe. 'On business. Last minute. It won't happen again.'

She shot a quick look at Alex, whose face had turned even stonier. 'I'll organise a press conference as soon as possible and we'll sort this out. Jo,' she said with more confidence than she felt, 'you've come a long way since then. It'll be OK.'

Alex had barely been able to resist the urge to hurl the paper against the wall when he'd read the article. The only part they'd left out was that Jo's ex-boyfriend had been his business partner. A man he thought he'd known inside out. His best friend. Who'd nearly destroyed Jo and had nearly ruined him.

He kept his gaze fixed on his sister and battled the shock that she'd so casually let slip to Mark something he'd taken such pains to keep buried. Hadn't she learned from him? Hadn't he warned her about the dangers of trusting people? About what happened if you let someone get near you?

Alex's hands clenched into fists and he had to stamp down on the urge to hunt Mark down and beat him to a pulp. The night of the pre-launch party slammed into his head. The threats and the warnings as he'd dragged Mark out of the pond that he'd dismissed as drunken ramblings. The debts. All tiny little clues that Mark might be a danger. And he'd ignored them.

The moment he'd seen the headlines, guilt had started attacking him on all sides. Firstly for failing to protect Jo. Again. A second blast had struck him when he'd realised that Jo had needed him and he hadn't been there. As if that hadn't been enough for one man in one lifetime, guilt also prickled that he'd lured Phoebe away for the weekend when she ought to have been here for his sister.

He glanced over at her and there it was again, another arrow of guilt piercing his chest. Because despite the torment his sister was suffering, the main thought rattling round his brain was how soon he could get Phoebe back into his bed.

A wave of weariness swept through him. He'd been carrying around the burden of guilt for five years now. It had clung to his shoulders like a heavy mantle, dragging him down, and he was so tired of it.

His gaze flickered over to his sister. She was listening to Phoebe outlining the strategy for sorting out the mess, and it struck him that she seemed a lot calmer and more confident than he'd have imagined in the circumstances. In fact she appeared to be more concerned with the effect that Mark's revelations might have on her career rather than on her personally.

Phoebe was right, he realised with something of a shock. Jo had come a long way since then. She didn't need him to pick up the pieces any longer. So why was he still beating himself up over something that Jo had clearly decided to get over?

Would it really be so bad if he dispensed with the guilt? Jo had told him time and time again that she didn't hold him in any way responsible for what had happened to her, but up until now he had resolutely resisted the temptation to forgive himself. And what good was that doing anyone?

Jo might have come a long way, but he hadn't, he acknowledged reluctantly. If his sister was able to get over what had happened and get on with things, why shouldn't he?

CHAPTER ELEVEN

Jo AND THE last of the journalists left the room where the press conference had been held and Phoebe slumped back into her chair.

Thank God. It was over and she never wanted to go through anything like it again. She could scarcely believe how close she'd come to losing everything. She felt dizzy just thinking about it.

But she'd pulled it off. She'd spent the last twenty-four hours working like a demon with her phone permanently glued to her ear while she slowly repaired their reputations. And it had paid off. Jo had been brilliant and the fashion house deal was back on.

Phoebe herself was back in control and she didn't intend to lose it again. Ever. If that meant no more hot sex with Alex, then so be it.

She ignored the little voice in her head telling her she was a fool to let something so fantastic go. But it was only sex, and she couldn't afford to slip up again. The way she'd been so out of control on Saturday night, so at the mercy of her body's needs, terrified her and she wanted no more of it.

She might not be able to avoid Alex altogether, she

thought, folding her arms on the table and resting her forehead on them, but she could certainly make sure she never slept with him again.

Alex strode back into the hotel conference room and cleared his throat. Phoebe jumped and jerked back. 'You look like you could do with this,' he said, placing a cup of coffee in front of her.

That was an understatement. Phoebe looked awful. Dark circles ringed her eyes and her face was pale.

'Oh. Er, thanks. I didn't see you earlier.'

He sat on the edge of the table and watched her carefully. 'I was lurking at the back. Congratulations.'

'Thank you.' She gave him a wan smile. 'And thank you for keeping out of things.'

Alex lifted a shoulder. 'It was part of the deal. Have you missed me?'

Phoebe's gaze snapped to his face. 'No,' she said quickly, and then began to shuffle the papers on the table.

Alex grinned. 'What are you doing for the rest of the afternoon?'

'Work, I imagine.'

'You ought to get some rest.' Preferably in his bed.

'I ought to get going.'

'Do you ever stop?'

'At the moment I can't afford to stop,' she said with a brief humourless smile that made him frown. 'You've been involved with new businesses. You must know that they require attention every hour of the day and night.'

True. And investing in new businesses meant a similar kind of commitment. But Alex recognised the signs of exhaustion and the way Phoebe was going she'd collapse before long.

'Would you like a lift?'

A startled look of horror crossed her face. Surely his suggestion wasn't that bad? But if that was her reaction to a lift, maybe he'd wait until she was in a more relaxed frame of mind before putting forward his proposal that they continue to see each other. 'No. It's fine. I can get a taxi.'

'You'll never find one. It's pouring outside.'

'Or a bus or a train or something.'

Her cool tone and the way she deliberately avoided eye contact was beginning to irritate him. As was the incessant shuffling of papers. What was the matter with her? Alex crossed his arms over his chest. 'Is something wrong?'

'Wrong?' Her gaze flicked to his for a second and then darted away. 'The press conference went well and Jo's career is back on track. What could possibly be wrong?'

The ball of baffled frustration that had been ricocheting around his chest stopped and burst. To hell with waiting. 'How about the fact that only a couple of days ago you were writhing in my arms, gasping with pleasure and begging me for more, yet now you can't wait to see the back of me?'

Colour stained her cheeks and her gaze slid to the table. 'That was then.'

'What's changed?'

'What happened on the island was a one off.' She sighed and when she did finally deign to look at him her eyes were unfathomable and Alex found he didn't like it one little bit. 'A momentary lapse of reason. It was a mistake.' She plucked her jacket off the back of her chair.

'So I guess an affair's out of the question,' he drawled.

Phoebe went very still. 'An affair?'

'You and me and the hot sex you were so keen on on Saturday night.'

She threaded her arms through her jacket and did the buttons up. 'You're right. Totally out of the question. I'm not interested in an affair.'

Disappointment far greater than it should have been thwacked him in the stomach. Then just before she twisted away he saw that her hands were trembling and it made him wonder. 'So you don't want me?'

'No, I don't. Not any more.'

He slid off the table and moved closer. 'And you don't want me to pull you into my arms right now and kiss you until you're shaking with desire? You don't want me to peel that little suit off you and spread you over the table and trail my mouth over every inch of your body?'

'No.' Her voice cracked.

'In that case you definitely won't want me doing this.'

Alex spun her round and brought his mouth down on hers. His arms snapped round her and he pulled her tight against him. He plunged his tongue into her mouth and desire flared inside him. His heart hammered. But Phoebe remained rigid in his punishing embrace.

He broke off, breathing raggedly, and stared down at her. 'Kiss me back,' he muttered hoarsely.

'No,' she said, glaring at him, fury written all over her face.

God, why was she denying this? Did she really not want him? The thought made him dizzy for a second. It was an uncomfortable sensation. But maybe she didn't. Maybe he'd read it all wrong and Saturday night had just been about high-running tempers. If that was the case then he had no business hauling her about, however much he might want to.

He was just about to let her go when he saw something flicker in the depths of her eyes. His heart skidded to a halt. She did want him. Triumph and relief pummelled through him.

He'd make her respond, make her see that an affair was an excellent idea, if it was the last thing he did. He loosened his grip on her and slid one hand slowly up her back to her neck and buried his fingers in her hair.

Alex felt her tense as if in preparation for another onslaught, but when he lowered his head this time he brushed his lips against hers and then dropped feather light kisses along her jaw.

Phoebe's head dropped back and he smiled against her skin. He explored the creamy smoothness of her neck and then found her mouth again and this time when he kissed her he found no resistance. Just warm, wet sweetness.

'If you don't want me,' he murmured, 'then this is the moment when you would slap me.'

Phoebe jerked back and without warning her hand flew up. She was quick but Alex's instincts were quicker. With a sharp curse he blocked her hand and wrapped his fingers around her wrist.

'What was that for?' he said, his eyes blazing.

'You suggested it.'

Alex stared at her, stunned. He'd felt less at sea in the middle of the ocean in the throes of a force-twelve hurricane. 'You want me.'

'No, I don't.'

He'd had enough. 'I thought *I* was good at denial but you're a master. You'd drive a man to drink.'

'All right,' yelled Phoebe. 'I do want you. You're right. Saturday night was amazing. I do want a repeat. But it's not going to happen.'

Alex shoved his hands through his hair. 'Why the hell not?'

She gaped. 'How can you even ask that? While I was in your bed, papers were going to print with that story. I should have been here.'

Alex froze. Was that what this was all about? Guilt? It was lucky he was an expert on the subject. 'That wasn't your fault. It was mine. I shouldn't have dragged you off to the island in the first place.'

'I could have got on that boat. I *should* have got on that boat.'

Alex frowned. 'It wouldn't have made any difference. We were due to leave at lunchtime.'

Phoebe threw her hands up in a gesture of anguish. 'I'd planned to hitch a lift with one of your colleagues who was leaving that night. If I'd done that, if I'd had the strength to stick to the plan I would have been here for Jo.' She laughed bitterly. 'But no. What did I do? Leap into bed with you.'

He winced at the disgust in her voice even though he knew it was directed more at herself than at him. 'Guilt doesn't do anyone any good. It's a complete waste of time.'

'Hah. What would you know about guilt? I bet you've never suffered a moment's guilt in your entire life.'

Alex felt as if she'd thumped him in the gut. 'Is that what you think? Then let me set you straight. I've spent the last five years riddled with guilt. Over what happened to Jo. Over whether I could have done something to prevent it. And you know what? Maybe I could have done more. Who knows? But one thing I've come to realise recently is that beating yourself up about something that can't be undone is utterly pointless.'

'It isn't pointless,' she said sharply. 'It can stop you making the same mistake again.'

'Can it? Does it stop *you* making the same mistakes again?'

Phoebe glared at him. 'It'll stop me jumping into bed with you again.'

Alex reeled. 'I didn't realise you found it so unpleasant the first time.'

Her shoulders dropped and she ran a hand through her hair. 'I didn't. You know I didn't. But you make me lose control. You distort my focus. My judgement does derail when I get distracted and I can't risk that.' Her voice cracked. 'Honestly, sometimes I feel like my finger is hovering over my self-destruct button and it's only sheer will power that stops me from jabbing at it and watching my life unravel with some sort of morbidly fascinating relief. I nearly just lost everything. My business, my career, everything I've ever worked for.' She pulled her shoulders back and shot him a look of calm finality. 'I won't compromise that for a brief fling with you. It's just not worth it.'

Something deep inside Alex suddenly exploded. 'That's utter rubbish.'

'*What?*' Phoebe gasped but he carried on regardless.

'You're good at your job. You know you are. You spent long enough telling me about it. You might not have been available the instant the story hit the papers, but you salvaged the situation regardless.'

'By the skin of my teeth.'

'But you did it. And if you're so terrified of your precious life unravelling, why set up your own business when nine out of ten start-ups fail within the first year? Now I have no idea where this sudden misguided lack of confidence comes from, or even if it *is* a sudden mis-guided lack of confidence, but whatever it is, for some reason I can't work out, you're using it to hide behind.'

'I'm not hiding behind anything. Is it really so difficult to believe that I just don't want to have an affair with you?'

'Frankly, yes. Because your body still craves mine as much as mine craves yours.'

Phoebe shrugged as if electrifying sexual chemistry was nothing more than a minor inconvenience in her life. 'That's just biology.'

Alex felt the energy drain out of him. Why was he fighting so hard for this? It wasn't as if Phoebe were the only woman on the planet. 'Fine.' He stepped back and shot her a humourless smile. 'You know some-thing? I really don't need the hassle. I just thought a fling might be fun.'

And with that he turned on his heel and stormed out.

CHAPTER TWELVE

THE MINUTE PHOEBE got home, the strain of holding herself together snapped. The door slammed behind her and her bag landed on the hall floor with a thud. Her raincoat fell into a crumpled heap a foot further on and she stumbled into the sitting room. Her legs gave way and she collapsed on the sofa shaking uncontrollably.

The taunts and accusations Alex had hurled at her spun round and round inside her head so relentlessly that she wished she could reach in and yank them out.

Because he didn't know her. He couldn't know the effect her upbringing had had on her. Nor the power of the rigid principles that her parents had instilled in her. He couldn't possibly understand the stress of living with the fear that of all the siblings she was the one most likely to let everyone down. Unless she kept a firm grip on her emotions that could happen all too easily.

So Alex was wrong. She wasn't hiding. It was all about self-preservation, mainly saving herself from herself. He had no right to have a go at her like that.

And yet...

The little voice that had been hammering away at

her conscience throughout the Tube journey refused to be silenced.

What if Alex was right?

Phoebe sat up, crossed her legs and pulled a cushion onto her lap. What if she *was* using her insecurities as an excuse and hiding behind a wall of guilt?

She'd survived the past couple of days, hadn't she? She hadn't let anyone down, least of all her family.

And actually guilt didn't stop the same mistakes happening over again, did it? Not when other emotions came into play and corrupted your ability to think rationally.

Guilt certainly didn't prevent problems and tricky situations sprouting up all over the place. And what was she going to do when they did? Torment herself with 'what if's and 'if only's and 'should have's? Or just get on and deal with them?

Frankly she was always going to fret about any course of action she took and wonder whether things might have turned out better had she done something differently. It was the way she was built and had been for the last twenty-nine years. She might as well get used to it.

Phoebe chewed on her lip. She tentatively ran her mind back over the conversation with Alex in the conference room and tried to look at it from his point of view. All he'd done was suggest an affair and she'd completely overreacted. Her cheeks burned and she buried her face in the cushion.

What was so scary about an affair anyway? People had them all the time without going to pieces. After all, it wasn't even as if Alex had been proposing a proper relationship. Just sex to unwind after a long day at work. Stringless, emotionless but scorching nonetheless.

Fun, he'd said. An affair with Alex wouldn't just be

fun. It would be amazing. Exhilarating. And probably
about time. She'd worked hard, but it had been at the
expense of playing, and didn't she deserve some fun?

Surely she'd be able to keep her focus clear. She was
a very different person from the infatuated fool she'd
been when Dillon had betrayed her three years ago.
And what was she going to do? Steer clear of men and
messy emotion for ever?

As her brain adjusted to the possibility of an affair
with Alex Phoebe felt excitement flicker in her breast. She
had no plans for the afternoon and she was far too wound
up to settle down to work. She ought to dash over to his
office right now and tell him of her change of mind.

Hmm. In all likelihood he'd never want to see her
again. She'd resisted him. Rejected him. She'd nearly
slapped him, for heaven's sake. Shame hit her square in
the chest. That had been particularly appalling. She
owed him an apology for that at the very least.

Because she *had* wanted him. He'd definitely been
right about that. She'd wanted him with an urgency that
confounded her but had her heart thundering just
thinking about it now. When he'd described what he'd
like to do to her on the table in the conference room
she'd nearly passed out at the thrill.

Phoebe jumped up as the glimmer of an idea crept
into her head. Maybe there was a way she could let him
know she'd changed her mind without actually having
to suffer the embarrassment of admitting that maybe,
just maybe, he was right and she'd been wrong.

After all, didn't actions speak louder than words?

Alex sat back in his chair and tried to concentrate on the
meeting going on around him. Negotiations with his

latest investment opportunity were at a delicate stage. He ought to be dedicating his full attention to it.

But all he could think of was Phoebe's flat refusal to have an affair with him. The disdain in her voice, the look of horror on her face... It grated more than it should have. He never usually had any trouble persuading women into his bed.

Although there hadn't been too many of those lately.

Maybe that was why her rejection stung.

'Alex?'

The voice of one of his finance department snapped him out of his thoughts. 'What?'

'They're pushing for twenty-five percent. I know we originally wanted a fifty-percent stake, but I think we should drop it.'

'Settle at forty,' Alex said and suddenly got to his feet.

This was driving him insane. And dammit, there was no reason he should feel like this. His scowl deepened with every stride towards his office. Where was his address book? He threw himself into his chair and pulled out the drawers of his desk. Aha.

Alex brushed off the dust and flicked through yellowing pages filled with the phone numbers of women he'd dated over the years. One of the numbers was bound to still be valid. He didn't particularly care which one. Any of them would do to prove to himself he didn't need Phoebe.

His phone rang and he snatched it up. 'What?' he barked and then told himself to calm down. Whatever his frustrations, they had nothing to do with his secretary.

'I have a Ms Jackson to see you.'

Alex nearly dropped the phone. Then his eyes narrowed and he felt himself grow cold. What was she here for? Wasn't rejecting him bad enough? Was she now planning to slap a sexual harassment charge on him as well?

He had every intention of telling his secretary to tell Phoebe to get lost, so he was utterly stunned to hear the words, 'Show her in,' coming out of his mouth.

Alex clenched his fists and moved round to stand in front of his desk where he reckoned he'd look more intimidating and more in control. And if ever he needed to be in control, now, with his brain behaving like a loose cannon, was it.

The firm rap at his door made his pulse spike.

'Come in,' he said curtly.

The door swung open slowly and Phoebe sidled in. Something about the way she moved had every one of his senses springing to attention.

Unable to help himself, he let his gaze travel over her. Her hair was tied back but she'd done something to her eyes. They seemed bigger than he recalled, more slumberous somehow. Her mouth seemed...poutier.

Alex swallowed and dragged his gaze over the rest of her. She was wearing the knee-length raincoat she'd had on earlier—with the collar turned up and the belt tightly tied around her waist—but she'd changed her shoes. If she'd been wearing those black patent heels at the press conference he'd have remembered. As he'd have remembered the inches of leg enclosed in sheer black nylon.

'You'll have to be quick,' he said, hauling his gaze back up to her face. 'I'm in the middle of a meeting.'

'So your secretary said. I don't mind waiting.'

Was it his imagination or had her voice dropped a couple of notes? 'Fine. What can I do for you?'

A slow smile curved her lips. 'It's really more a question of what I can do for you.'

Alex's mouth went dry and his body temperature shot up as an image of exactly what she could do for him slammed into his head. So much for thinking he was in control. He needed to sit down before the effect she was having on him became too obvious. Deliberately taking his time, he levered himself off the edge of his desk and moved to sit behind it. At least her legs were now out of sight, not that that offered much comfort to his aching body.

'And what is that?' He picked up a pencil and began to twirl it around his fingers as if he couldn't be less bothered by her presence in his office.

'I've come to apologise.'

Alex's brain had clearly disintegrated because he hadn't the faintest idea of what she was talking about. 'What for?'

'Slapping you.'

'You didn't.'

'I wanted to.'

'Why?'

'You suggested an affair.'

'You turned me down.'

She reached up and pulled the band from her hair. Glossy curls tumbled over her shoulders. 'I've changed my mind.'

Alex's pulse leapt. 'How predictable,' he drawled.

Phoebe's smile faltered for a split second but she didn't take her eyes off him. 'I thought you might say that.'

She took her hands out of her pockets and unknotted her belt. Then she started to undo the buttons. Achingly slowly. The lapels fell open revealing a V of skin and a tantalising glimpse of black lace.

The scorching heat of her gaze trapped him where he sat. Alex couldn't move. He could barely breathe.

'I also wanted to say that I've had time to reflect on the points you mentioned and have come to the conclusion you might be right.'

'About what?' He cleared his throat.

'A number of things, but mainly the futility of guilt.'

'I see,' he said hoarsely, thinking that that was utter rubbish. All he could see was Phoebe.

'Did you really feel that guilty about what happened to Jo?'

Alex blinked. 'It consumed me day and night.'

'Past tense?'

'Absolutely.'

'Good, because she doesn't blame you, you know.'

'I know.'

'So blaming yourself is pointless.'

'I know.'

'Based on that reasoning I now see I may have been a bit hasty in rejecting your proposal.'

The pencil snapped.

Her smile deepened and she walked round the desk. 'If you're still open to the idea, I don't see any reason why we shouldn't have an affair.'

His chair swivelled as he followed her every move. Hunger and desire roared along his veins and his erection strained and ached. 'I'm still open to the idea.'

Then she was standing in front of him, her coat hanging open, baring soft skin and black lace and those shoes, and Alex's vision blurred. 'Earlier this afternoon you mentioned something about peeling my clothes off, spreading me out over a table and trailing your mouth over every inch of my body.'

Had he? That sounded like the best idea he'd had in a long time.

Phoebe sat on his lap and leaned forward to whisper in his ear. 'I've done the first bit. How about you helping me with the rest?'

Her scent spun through his head and the last vestige of control snapped. He clamped one arm around her waist to keep her where she was and reached for the phone with the other. He pressed the button that connected to his secretary's desk. 'Cancel my appointments for the rest of the day and take the afternoon off,' he said when she answered. 'Something's come up.'

Alex hung up and Phoebe let out a soft laugh. 'Thank goodness for that. I thought you were going to call Security.'

He raised an eyebrow and smiled. 'Why would I want to do a thing like that when you're apologising so nicely?'

Phoebe gripped the back of his chair, lowered her mouth to his and kissed him so slowly and thoroughly that Alex's head swam. As her tongue slid along his, his hands delved beneath the lapels of her coat and gently pushed it down her arms. She shrugged it off and then wound her arms around his neck and pressed her pelvis against his. She moaned into his mouth and Alex lost it.

With one quick move he wiped the papers and pens and things off his desk and lifted her onto it. Her coat fell to the floor. Phoebe untangled her hands from his hair and eased herself back onto the leather.

Alex stared down at her and thought he'd never seen anything so beautiful. The bra she was wearing was a strapless concoction of lace and silk that pushed her breasts up and out. Further down, she wore a matching suspender belt and the tiniest excuse for knickers he'd ever come across.

The blood roared in his ears and then he found he could barely think. Only act. He unclipped her bra and slipped it off her and her breasts spilled free. He ran his hands over the rounded flesh and rubbed his thumbs over her nipples. Phoebe gasped sharply and arched her back as if begging him to take them in his mouth. Alex leaned down and trailed a string of feather light kisses over the sensitive skin of her chest before flicking his tongue over the straining nub.

'Oh, God, don't stop,' she whispered raggedly. 'Don't ever stop.'

Alex didn't plan on stopping. He lifted his head for a second to gaze down into her face. Her cheeks were flushed and she was biting into her lip as if trying to stop herself from crying out.

He kissed his way down the soft skin of her stomach and pressed his mouth to the hot wet heat of her. Phoebe jerked as if he'd branded her.

Alex's fingers shook as he hooked them under the thin lace at her hips and pulled her panties down her legs. His hands circled her ankles, slid up her shins, swept up her inner thighs and her legs fell apart.

His hands moved round to cup her bottom, then lifted her to his mouth. Her hips automatically tried to twist but he held them down. He pressed his thumb against her clitoris and she groaned.

Then his mouth was on her, licking and sucking and tasting with just enough pressure to drive her wild. He felt her tremble, heard her breathing shallow and, as he licked deeper inside her, felt her tense and then shatter. His mouth pressed against her, absorbing every tremor shuddering through her, milking every drop of her desire. Eventually, when the aftershocks subsided, he kissed his way up her body, feeling every tiny nerve ending of her skin jumping as he did so.

Alex planted his hands either side of her and leaned over her. Her face was flushed, and her eyes a dark shimmering green. A satisfied grin spread across her face and Alex felt something shift deep inside him. 'This was supposed to be about what I could do for you,' Phoebe murmured.

'Too late. Every time I sit at this desk,' he said hoarsely, 'I'm going to see you. Like this. It's going to be agony.'

She pushed herself up on her elbows and gave him a slow smile. 'Well, we can't have that, can we?'

Her eyes dropped to the huge bulge in his trousers and widened. He was so hard he ached and he was seconds away from unzipping his fly and plunging straight into her without a thought for the consequences.

Stunned by the ferocity of his desire Alex jerked back and removed himself from temptation. The taste of her on his tongue had addled his brain.

Phoebe slithered off the desk and reached for her coat. 'Is this what you're looking for?' she said, delving into the pocket and pulling out a condom.

Too right. He lunged for her but she dodged him, instead backing away in the direction of the sofa, a come-hither look in her eye that he couldn't have resisted even if he'd wanted to.

Alex matched her pace for pace, not breaking eye contact with her for a second. He ripped his clothes off and tossed them to the floor. Phoebe slipped out of her shoes and suspender belt and rolled down her stockings, her teeth digging into her lower lip and her steps becoming more and more languid until she stopped altogether.

Alex didn't stop. He'd never seen anything lovelier. Taking the condom out of her trembling hands, he shoved one hand in her hair and kissed her hard, twisting her around and pulling her down with him onto the sofa.

Phoebe sprawled on top of him, her breasts crushing against his chest. His hands stroked over the backs of her thighs and up over her bottom and she moaned into his mouth.

In one quick powerful move, he tipped her off the sofa and onto the rug. As his hands and mouth roamed over her Phoebe's soft, stunned laughter soon turned to moans of pleasure. Slipping a finger deep inside her, he watched her writhe and gasp and arch her back. And when she was convulsing around him, crying out his name Alex lifted himself over her and drove into her.

A fever raged inside him as he saw her eyes widen and felt her muscles clamp around his length. Her legs wound round his waist as if she never wanted to let him go. Her nails raked his back as between pants she told him exactly how he was making her feel.

Her hips rose to meet every thrust in perfect synchronicity. Alex's heart hammered. The blood thundered around his body and pleasure pounded along his veins. No one had ever made him lose control like this. As his head went blank of everything except pure need Alex gave in and let his body take over. His thrusts quickened, intensified, became harder and faster. He felt her tense and then shatter in his arms, and as waves of ecstasy slammed through him Alex plunged deep inside her, buried his face in her neck and with a great groan hit the strongest, most intense climax of his life.

They lay there together for a few moments while their breathing slowed then Alex rolled onto his back and pulled Phoebe with him.

'Have dinner with me tonight.'

She rested her chin on his chest. 'I can't.' She sighed and he felt it reverberate through him. 'My parents are having a party. They have it every year. For the great and good of the city. It's a nightmare.'

Alex waited for her to ask him to go with her and wondered how he'd say no. When she didn't it annoyed him. Which irritated him even more. He ought to be delighted that she understood the no-strings rule, but bizarrely he found himself wanting to know what her family was like. What sort of people had shaped the woman she was. 'Some other time perhaps.'

'That would be nice.'

If she wasn't going to invite him he'd have to get there some other way. 'What time do you have to be there?'

Phoebe picked up his wrist and glanced at his watch. 'In a couple of hours. I ought to go.'

She started to wriggle away, but Alex flung an arm around her to stop her going anywhere. He felt himself stirring inside her and her eyes widened. 'I'm not sure you're done apologising,' he said and tugged her head down for a kiss.

CHAPTER THIRTEEN

PHOEBE STEPPED OUT of the taxi and looked up at her parents' house with a familiar feeling of misgiving. Even the afterglow of this afternoon couldn't wipe out the ribbon of trepidation that wound through her.

And what an afternoon… How she'd ever plucked up the courage to turn up at Alex's office dressed like that she'd never know. Throughout the taxi ride she'd been convinced the driver had known exactly what she was up to. But it had certainly paid off. Phoebe went dizzy for a second as a flush swept up through her body and she had to clutch onto the railing for balance.

It had been on the tip of her tongue to invite him tonight, but she'd thought about the definition and general properties of a fling just in time and had bitten back the words. So she was on her own. As usual. It had never bothered her before, so why was it bothering her now?

Taking a deep breath and telling herself not to be so idiotic, she pulled her shoulders back and walked up the steps. The glossy black door swung open and a wall of warmth and chatter hit her. She smiled at the waiter and handed him her coat then wandered into the drawing room and started to squeeze her way through the guests.

With any luck she could say a speedy hello to her parents, avoid her siblings and leave after half an hour.

She'd start with her mother. Phoebe spied her by the fireplace and made her way over, feeling tension seep into her with every step.

'Hi, Mum,' she said, giving her mother a quick kiss on the cheek and bracing herself for an attack.

'You're late.'

'You look nice.'

'Thank you. So do you.' Her mother cast a critical eye over her outfit and nodded with approval. 'Good. There's someone I'd like you to meet.'

Oh, no. Not another one of her mother's attempts to get her to switch careers. Other people's mothers engaged in not-so-subtle efforts to marry off their daughters. But not her mother. She'd apparently made it her lifelong mission to rescue her daughter from the clutches of the frothy world of PR by any means possible. 'He's a friend of Dan's. Try and be nice.'

Phoebe fought the urge to stamp her foot like a petulant child and bleat that she didn't want to be nice and she didn't need to meet another man who thought he could whip her off the PR track and set her on the straight and narrow. But her mother had a firm grip on her arm and Phoebe was left with no choice but to follow.

Five minutes. That was all she'd give whoever her mother had lined up for her, and then she'd leave. She'd shown her face and that would have to do. All she wanted was to go home and flop into bed and relive the glorious hours she'd spent in Alex's office.

Phoebe fixed a bland smile to her face and rummaged around in her head for her stash of stock responses.

'Here we are.'

She glanced round to where her mother was looking and her jaw dropped. She'd recognise that back anywhere. Only an hour ago she'd been raking her nails all over it.

Alex turned and a bubble of delight started bouncing around inside her. What on earth was he doing here?

'Phoebe, this is Alex Gilbert. He's a venture capitalist. Alex, this is my daughter Phoebe. She's in PR.' Her mother scrunched her nose up. 'But I'm hoping you might be able to make her see the light.'

'I'm delighted to meet you,' he said softly, a smile hovering at his lips. He dropped a kiss on her cheek and she swayed as she breathed in his scent.

'Me too.' Her voice sounded husky and she cleared her throat.

'Perhaps some of you will rub off on her.'

'I'll try and make sure that it does.'

Phoebe felt her cheeks flame. God, he was gorgeous. Dressed in a navy suit and pale blue shirt he looked dark and dishevelled and Phoebe felt her heart lurch.

'Remember. Rub.' Her mother patted him on the arm and made a little circular movement with her hand.

'How could I forget?'

Her mother blushed and giggled, then dashed off muttering, 'Charming. Quite charming.'

Phoebe stood there stunned. Since when had her mother blushed and giggled? 'Alex,' she said, when she eventually managed to find her voice. 'Gatecrashing again?'

Alex grinned. 'Why do you automatically assume that I receive so few invitations that I have to gatecrash parties?'

'You mean you actually have an invitation?'

'I do.'

'Who from?'

'Your brother.'

'Why didn't you mention it earlier when we—?' She broke off and went red.

'I didn't have it then. I rang your brother after I dropped you home.'

'Why?'

Alex shrugged and frowned slightly as if he couldn't work it out either. 'I was intrigued.'

'By what?'

'Your family. They sounded interesting.'

'You think?' she said, her eyebrows shooting up.

'Perhaps "interesting" isn't the right word. Your mother I'd describe as a force to be reckoned with.'

He sounded as if he thought that was a good thing. 'She's a Rottweiler in couture.'

Alex laughed. 'She's been telling me all about you.'

That really didn't sound good.

'Would you like to know what she said?'

Alex was standing so close she could feel the warmth coming off his body and she swayed involuntarily towards him. His gaze roamed over her face as if he was trying to memorise every millimetre. Phoebe's mouth went dry and her surroundings faded until all that she was aware of was a hot flame of desire burning deep inside her and a desperate need to kiss him.

'Not really,' she breathed, staring at his mouth. 'I'd much rather—'

'Hello, Ditz, darling.'

Phoebe jumped as the strident voice of her sister pierced the bubble that had enveloped them. She blinked as if coming out of a trance and caught the amused quizzical expression on his face. 'Ditz?' he murmured.

Phoebe couldn't believe it. Why now? After all these years?

'Family nickname,' she mumbled. 'A very, very *old* family nickname,' she added, swinging round and glaring at Camilla.

'Now that's something your mother didn't mention,' Alex said with a grin.

'Probably because most of us have forgotten about it. Haven't we?' she said pointedly to her sister.

But Camilla wasn't paying any attention. Instead she was staring at Alex with undisguised admiration. 'Who's this?'

Phoebe performed the introductions and watched as her sister gave Alex one of her most dazzling smiles before turning back to Phoebe.

'So how's the fluffy world of PR?'

Ah, how long had that taken? Thirty seconds? Camilla was slipping.

'Still fluffy.' She'd long since given up trying to justify what she did to her family. 'How's the matter-of-life-and-death world of cardiac surgery?'

'Busy. They're making me Head of Department.'

'Wow, congratulations.'

Camilla grinned. 'Thanks. Of course, it's going to be mad. So much pressure.' She laughed and shrugged and batted her eyelids in Alex's direction. 'You know sometimes I wish I had a job like Phoebe's. All glamour and long lunches. Parties and celebrities and gorgeous shoes.'

Phoebe felt the old familiar feeling of hurt swell up inside her. Calm down, she told herself. She doesn't mean it. She forced herself to smile and opened her mouth to mumble some sort of agreement.

'Actually, it's not all long lunches and parties, is it,

Phoebe?' Alex's voice sounded mild but she cast a quick astonished glance at him, and saw that his jaw had tightened and if anything he looked even bigger and taller than she remembered.

'What? Oh—er—no.'

'Are you in the same field?' asked Camilla.

'No. But I've seen her in action. And it's extremely hard work. Everyone only sees the results. They don't see the hours of effort put in. The constant juggling, the management, the organisation.' He smiled lazily but the look in his eye was razor sharp. 'It might not look like life and death, but reputations can hang in the balance and the way the balance goes can have a serious impact on those involved.'

Crikey. Even Phoebe was now seriously impressed by what she did.

His eyes pinned Camilla to the spot as he continued his ruthless attack. 'And who do you think it is who comes to the rescue of hospitals when a story appears about a patient dying on the operating table, or some misdemeanour during routine surgery?'

Was her ice-cool sister actually blushing?

'Yes—er—I see what you mean.'

'From my own experience Phoebe has been first class.' He shot her a look that curled her toes. Which particular experience was he talking about?

'My sister was about to lose everything.'

Good, the professional one. Not the personal one. Not the hot and steamy and fiery one. Excellent. Wasn't it?

Phoebe gave up trying to work out what she thought she ought to be thinking and decided to just wallow in his praise. Who knew when she'd get another chance?

'Phoebe worked her guts out to protect her reputation and restore her confidence and fix the problem. She pulled off an incredible piece of damage limitation when I wouldn't have had a clue what to do. And as the balance tipping the wrong way could well have sent my sister spiralling down into hell, I do rather consider it to be a matter of life and death.'

'Yes, well, she's always been the brightest one in the family.'

Phoebe's jaw dropped.

'Well, you are,' said Camilla tetchily. 'Oh, the rest of us might have the doctorates or the string of letters after our names, but you're the creative one, the only one who has any sort of emotional intelligence. To tell you the truth I'm rather envious.'

Whatever next? Would her father renounce all things capitalist and take up yoga?

'Right, who'd like a drink?' said Alex.

'God, yes, please,' said Phoebe with more haste than decorum.

Alex nodded and gave her a scorching smile. 'I'll be right back.' Then he turned on his heel.

'Wow,' said Camilla, staring at him with an unusually dazed expression on her face. 'I wouldn't mind having him on my side. He's quite something.'

'I wouldn't get too carried away,' Phoebe muttered, swirling with confusion and feeling all topsy-turvy inside. 'He probably bites the heads off Jelly Babies.'

As Alex stopped, turned and shot her a wicked grin Phoebe added 'hearing of a bat' to his list of talents. 'Actually,' he said, 'I swallow them whole.'

'Is she always like that?' asked Alex, thrusting a glass of champagne into Phoebe's hand and steering her through the French doors and into the relative peace of the garden.

'She doesn't mean it like it sounds,' said Phoebe, shrugging and following him into the shadows. 'I guess when you're doing something that saves lives, public relations does seem a little shallow.'

'Rubbish.'

'Well, I know that and you know that, but they're not as enlightened as we are.'

Alex dropped a swift hard kiss on her mouth that left her reeling. 'You are beautiful and brilliant. You look incredible in that dress, and you'd look even better out of it.'

Phoebe's heart thumped. 'Someone should bottle you.'

She took a sip of champagne. Did it really matter what her family thought of her job anyway? She'd been doing it for years. She was good at it and she loved it. If she'd been truly concerned she'd have given into the pressure and become a corporate lawyer years ago. She wasn't going to give up her career, so it was high time she got over her fear of letting them down.

'What happens to the people whose businesses fail, Alex?'

'Those that are determined enough pick themselves up and start again.'

'As simple as that?'

'It's far from simple, but it's what I did.'

'Really?' He'd lost everything? 'When?'

'A while ago. In the early days.'

'What happened?'

'I made a bad judgement call.'

'Nice to know it happens to you too.'

He gave her a small smile. 'Only once. That was enough. How about that dinner?'

'Sounds great.'

CHAPTER FOURTEEN

'ARE YOU GOING to sit behind that paper *all* morning?' Jo prodded the pages of Alex's paper and made reading the rest of the article on the new piece of technology launched by the latest company he'd invested in impossible.

'That was my plan.'

'I've hardly seen you all week.'

'I've been working.'

Her eyes held a mischievous light he didn't entirely trust. 'Evenings too?'

No. Alex had spent every evening since her parents' party with Phoebe. Most lunchtimes too. He couldn't seem to get enough of her. 'Some.'

'But you must have found time to eat? Take the air?'

He frowned. What was Jo talking about? He scoured her face but couldn't find anything other than mild curiosity in her expression. His sister obviously wanted to chat. Presumably that was why she'd suggested breakfast. And as he'd been keen to find out what spending time with his sister without being racked with guilt might be like, he'd agreed. So it was high time he started doing exactly that.

Suddenly realising he felt lighter than he had in

years, Alex grinned, folded the paper and set it on the table. 'Sorry. Bad habit. How are things coming along for the launch?'

'Brilliantly.' Jo beamed. 'I've finally finished the collection and there's not a drop of glue in sight.'

'Thank heavens for that.'

'I can't believe it's only a week away.'

'I'm very proud of you, you know.'

'I know. I'm kind of proud of me too. Although I couldn't have done it without Phoebe.'

'Probably not.'

'Hah,' said Jo triumphantly. 'You see. I told you she'd be brilliant. It's odd, though,' she added after a little pause, spooning sugar into the cup and idly stirring her coffee.

Alex waited for her to continue but Jo appeared to have gone off into her own little world. The relentless clink of her spoon against the side of the cup started to set his teeth on edge. 'What's odd?'

Jo blinked and looked up at him. 'She's different.'

Alex already knew that. Why else would he have broken the vow he'd made years ago never to see the same woman more than a couple of times? The fact that he'd not only broken it but hadn't wasted a moment agonising over it should have scared the living daylights out of him.

Instead, while he wasn't exactly shouting it from the rooftops, the idea of having Phoebe around a bit longer didn't have him running for the hills. In fact it made him feel warm and remarkably content. Especially when he thought about the delightful manner in which she'd woken him up this morning before telling him he ought to go home before she forgot where it was.

'Different in what way?' he said, taking care not to appear too interested in Jo's answer.

'She has a sort of spring in her step.'

'Does she?'

'I wonder what put it there.'

Alex's eyes narrowed in suspicion. This was no innocent conversation. 'What are you implying?'

'Me?' she said with breezy nonchalance. 'Nothing. But now that you mention it, I was wondering if it could have anything to do with this.'

Jo reached into her bag and dropped a magazine onto the table.

Alex raised an eyebrow and wondered where his sister was heading with this. 'A gossip magazine? I wouldn't have thought that was your sort of thing.'

'It wouldn't be normally. But when I hear that my brother is splashed all over it I suddenly find it essential reading. Pages six, seven, eight and nine.' Jo took a sip of coffee and grinned. 'Just for the record, because I know you don't need it, I approve.'

As he drew the magazine towards him wariness gripped him, and every one of his muscles tensed.

He flicked to the relevant section and as he began to read he felt the blood chill in his veins.

The headlines insinuating that the City's most eligible bachelor might finally have been snared by the current darling of the PR world swam before his eyes.

His heart pounding, he scanned the text and by the time he'd reached the final word the last flicker of warmth inside him died. Quotes littered the article. Phoebe was well aware of what he thought of journalists yet she'd obviously spoken to this one.

Alex knew his expression hadn't altered an inch. He'd perfected it to see him win out during the toughest negotiations. He'd never have thought he'd need to use it to conceal the winding effect of the crushing weight of betrayal.

A cold sweat broke out all over his skin as disillusionment and searing disappointment engulfed him. He pushed his chair back, not caring that all eyes in the cafe swivelled round at the grating sound of metal against stone.

'Alex?' Jo stared up at him in surprise, but he barely noticed.

Numbness started spreading through him, reaching out to wind itself around every cell of his body and gradually he began to feel absolutely nothing. 'I have to go.'

The last three days had been fabulous, Phoebe thought, taking the stack of papers and a steaming cup of coffee into the garden. A long delicious lazy dream and one she hoped she'd never have to wake up from. She'd signed up three new clients. She'd finalised the arrangements for Jo's launch. And she'd had more dynamite sex than she'd ever thought possible. She felt as if she were floating, which for a five foot nine generously proportioned woman was an unusual experience.

See, she told herself, aware that she was smiling smugly and not caring one little bit. Combining a fling with her career *was* possible. All it took was discipline and an ability to compartmentalise.

And the right man.

Alex, in fact.

Phoebe stopped suddenly in the middle of the patio and coffee slopped onto the stone. Uh oh. That didn't sound good. She put the papers and the mug on a table beside the sun lounger and tried to imagine not seeing Alex ever again. Not kissing him, not being able to stroke that magnificent body, not talking and laughing late into the night. Not having him deep inside her and sending her soaring.

Pain gripped her chest and her brain actually ached.

Oh, God, she had to watch it. She gave herself a quick shake and told herself not to be so stupid. There were bound to be hundreds of 'right' men out there. Thousands, even. What was the global population these days? Billions?

Phew. She had nothing to worry about. Alex was simply the right man for this particular stage in her life. That was all.

She'd barely finished the first article when the doorbell rang. With a sigh she dropped the newspaper on the grass and levered herself to her feet. How typical was that? Just when she'd been hoping for a stretch of uninterrupted peace and quiet in which to digest the papers and then gear herself up for meeting Alex later.

She padded through her house to the front door and peered through the spyhole. At the sight of Alex on her doorstep, her heart lurched and then galloped with delight. Had he not been able to wait until tonight?

Phoebe threw the door open and knew she ought to be playing it cool, but the idiotic smile she could feel curving her lips wasn't cool in the slightest.

However as she took in his dark, tight expression her smile faded and a flicker of alarm sprinted down her spine. Because the man looming on her doorstep with a thunderous look on his face and a fierce glint in his eyes bore little resemblance to the man who'd made love to her so thoroughly this morning.

'Alex? What's wrong?' When she'd left him, he'd been going to have breakfast with Jo. What could possibly have happened in the couple of hours since she'd last seen him?

Alex didn't answer, just barged his way into the hall and disappeared into the sitting room. Utterly bewildered, Phoebe raced after him and then slammed to a halt when she saw him standing, feet apart, with his back to the window, his massive frame radiating tension and fury.

'This is what's wrong,' he snarled and tossed a magazine on the table.

Phoebe stared at it as if it were a bomb he'd just dropped. Her heart sank. Oh, no. Please let it not be another story about Jo.

'It starts on page six.'

With trembling fingers Phoebe picked it up and swallowed back a surge of nausea. She didn't think Jo's career would survive another salacious story.

The pages were stuck together. Or maybe she was shaking so much it just seemed that way. But eventually she got to page six.

Her heart thumping with apprehension, Phoebe scanned the headline and her initial reaction was one of relief. Thank goodness. The story had nothing to do with Jo.

But as she read further the apprehension flooded back. The article was a dodgy blend of fact and supposition. About her and Alex. It detailed the times and location of their dates and hinted at the possible professional benefits such a relationship might give her. Indignation spiked through her alarm. As if she'd ever take advantage of their affair like that, even assuming that the supposed 'benefits' did exist.

Nevertheless it was awful. No wonder Alex was in such a foul mood. He hated any invasion of his privacy.

And those photos... Phoebe shuddered at the thought that someone had been watching them. As they kissed beneath the pergola at the roof gardens. While they were walking in the park during lunch a couple of days ago. In the middle of dinner at that cosy little Italian round the corner from his flat.

But even so, she thought, Alex must be used to seeing himself in the press, so why was he reacting so strongly about something that was so clearly fabricated and badly patched together?

'Nothing to say?'

Phoebe blinked and jumped in shock at the icy steel in his voice. 'Why would I have anything to say?'

'What? No hint of shame? No apology?'

She went very still. Confusion swilled around her head. 'What do I have to be ashamed of and what do I have to apologise for?' she said carefully.

Alex shoved his hands through his hair and let out a bitter laugh. 'You really are unbelievable.'

Phoebe gaped. What the hell was going on? 'Alex, I know how you feel about your privacy and I can imagine you're not particularly pleased about this—'

'Not particularly pleased?' he echoed, in a dangerously soft voice.

An inexplicable sense of dread seeped into her. 'Now you're scaring me.'

His eyes glittered and turned as dark and hard as granite. 'You tip the press off about our...' he paused as if searching for the right word '...our liaison,' he said eventually, 'and you accuse me of scaring you.'

'Is that what you think?' she said in horrified disbelief.

'It does seem a logical conclusion.'

'Why would I tip off the press about us?'

Alex's jaw tightened. 'I have no idea. Publicity? It wouldn't be the first time someone's used my name to bring in business.'

Phoebe felt the blood drain from her face. Her legs shook and she stumbled back, not stopping until she hit the bookcase. She gripped the edges and could feel her knuckles turning white with the effort of keeping herself upright. 'You arrogant bastard,' she breathed, scarcely unable to believe what was going on. 'Firstly, I don't need to use your name to bring in business. I'm doing exceptionally well by myself. And secondly, are you honestly suggesting I'd be capable of stooping that low?'

Alex glowered. 'You said yourself you'd do anything for your career.'

'Not this. Never something like this.'

'Read it again, Phoebe,' he said, picking up the magazine and thrusting it at her. 'You're quoted.'

How could she possibly be quoted? She hadn't spoken to anyone about her relationship with Alex, let alone a tabloid journalist.

She read it again, the words swimming before her eyes. And suddenly her shock gave way to anger. 'No, I'm not, you jerk. "A source close to Ms Jackson" does not mean me. It means they've made it up.'

'Right,' he said, his sarcasm striking her straight in the chest. 'And they'd do that because they're not worried about libel.'

Her anger turned into incandescence. 'This is a scandal sheet. They couldn't care less about libel. Their fabrications sell so many extra copies that they simply pay the injured parties off.'

'Do you seriously expect me to believe that?'

What? 'You should. It's the truth. But I suppose you think I lined the photographer up too.'

'It wouldn't surprise me.'

As Phoebe realised that Alex genuinely believed what he was saying she felt as if he'd thumped her in the stomach. Surely he must know she'd never go to the press with any information about him or their affair. So why was he doing this? And why did it hurt quite so much? The backs of her eyes stung and she swallowed back the lump in her throat. 'Don't you trust me at all?'

The look on Alex's face darkened and Phoebe felt her legs give way.

'Oh, my God,' she breathed in horror as she sank into an armchair. 'You don't, do you? You don't trust me an inch.'

A muscle throbbed in his jaw. 'It's nothing personal. I don't trust anyone.'

Nothing personal? *Nothing personal?* So why was her heart splintering? Why did she feel as if she were cracking open? She wanted to pummel him in the chest. Scratch his eyes out and pull him to pieces and hurt him as much as he was hurting her. 'Why not? What happened? Did an ex-girlfriend run to the press with a kiss and tell?'

'My ex-business partner ran to Bermuda with the contents of the company's bank account.'

Oh. Phoebe went very still.

'You once asked me about why I now work alone,' he bit out. 'Well, that's why.'

She could see that. But still… 'Alex, I'm not going to run off with your fortune.'

He raked his hands through his hair and his features suddenly twisted with such pain that Phoebe thought he was ill. And then his anger seemed to drain away and he looked wearier than she'd ever seen him. He slumped into a chair and rubbed a hand over his face.

'Rob was the boyfriend the article in the paper mentioned,' he said bleakly. 'The one who bullied Jo and put her into hospital.'

Oh, God. 'What happened?'

'We made a lot of money very quickly. I invested in property and other things. He spent a fortune on drugs and gambling.'

Alex's voice was flat, as if he were reciting the weather forecast. But his face was white and tight and she'd never seen such turmoil in his eyes.

'He met Jo and they started dating behind my back.'

Phoebe's heart squeezed and there wasn't a thing she could do to stop it. 'Why?'

Alex shrugged. 'She was sixteen. Rob was twenty-six. I guess they knew I wouldn't have approved. They went out for a year.' His voice cracked. 'A whole year and I didn't have a clue.'

Phoebe didn't know what to say. There was nothing she could say.

'The business was going through a rapid expansion and I was too engrossed to notice. Too focused on making money. I didn't notice how thin she was getting. And I didn't pay enough attention to Rob's increasingly erratic behaviour.'

No wonder he'd spent the last five years racked with guilt. Part of her wanted to jump up and take him in her arms. But the pain of his accusations was still too raw and she made herself stay where she was.

'I caught him slapping her once.'

Phoebe's hands flew to her mouth. 'What did you do?'

'I acquired a scar and the bump on my nose. Rob came off worse. He ended up in Casualty. A week later he disappeared and I discovered he'd cleared out our accounts.' He shrugged. 'I thought I knew him inside out. Turns out I didn't know him at all. So if I do have an issue with trust I think it's kind of understandable, don't you?'

Phoebe's heart wrenched. 'Absolutely. Five years ago. But now? Still?'

'It doesn't go away.'

'The guilt has.'

Alex frowned. 'Maybe.'

'I'm not Rob. I would never betray you, nor intentionally let you down.'

'You can't know that. I can't know that.'

Frustration suddenly flared inside her. Why was he being so stubborn about this? 'Well, like it or not, I think you do trust me.'

Alex tensed. 'I don't. I can't.'

'You can and you do. Why else would you have allowed me to work with Jo when all your instincts fought against it?'

'Because you were the best person for the job.'

'Has that ever influenced you in the past?'

'I don't allow my personal feelings to get in the way of business.'

Phoebe let out a hollow laugh. 'Really? I bet you've let that sense of betrayal influence every single decision you've made since.'

'I wouldn't be so short-sighted.'

'Yet you were so quick to think the worst of me.'

Alex went very still.

'You know,' Phoebe continued, chewing on her lip,

'I've made mistakes—plenty of them—but I've learned from them. Made myself stronger. You've let yours eat away at you. You once accused me of hiding, but who's hiding now?'

'I'm not hiding from anything.'

'Are you sure about that?'

'Absolutely.' Alex got to his feet and shrugged. 'Like I said, it's nothing personal.'

The cool indifference of his tone sliced through her and Phoebe felt as if a steel band had suddenly wrapped around her chest and were slowly crushing the air out of her lungs.

She'd thought she could handle this, that a casual fling was exactly what she wanted. But the power he had to wound her, the depth of the cut, told her more clearly than any number of words that she'd been fooling herself. She didn't want a mere fling. She wanted a proper relationship and she was convinced they'd been heading in that direction. But Alex clearly didn't.

Phoebe felt her heart harden. What an utter idiot she'd been. Well, not any more. 'If it's nothing personal,' she said quietly, 'then I think you should leave.'

Alex leaned back against the front door, closed his eyes and waited for relief to pour over him.

Because Phoebe was wrong. Utterly wrong. About everything. He didn't trust her. Or anyone. And so what if he *had* let the events of five years ago influence pretty much every decision he'd ever made? Look at the way Jo had turned out. And look at the way he'd picked himself up and rebuilt his fortune. Neither of those things would have happened if he'd allowed himself to trust anyone other than himself.

Even getting round to trusting himself, when he'd screwed up so spectacularly, had taken a heck of a lot of work. He'd had to shut himself off, hurl himself into some sort of emotional Siberia. Which was just fine. He was perfectly happy with that. Emotions were messy and he didn't need mess in his life ever again.

Alex pushed himself off the door and strode down the path. He couldn't afford to trust anyone. He'd never stand back and give anyone one hundred per cent autonomy. Never had and never would.

Except Phoebe.

He stopped, his hand on the gate, his heart suddenly pounding.

She'd been right. He did trust her. The realisation thundered into his head and with it came another flash of insight.

Maybe it was more than that.

One of the photos that accompanied the article flew into his head. He'd met Phoebe for lunch. They'd gone for a walk in the park. He'd slung his arm round her shoulders and they'd been laughing about something.

But it had been the look on his face and in his eyes that had put the fear of God into him. And then when he'd thought she'd betrayed him, he'd felt as if he'd been punched with such force he'd reeled back and crashed against the wall.

Suddenly something inside him collapsed. He was so tired of being cold, of not allowing himself to feel. He was tired of empty, meaningless flings. What he had with Phoebe wasn't empty or meaningless. He'd shared more with her in the past week both emotionally and physically than he had with anyone ever before.

And he'd just thrown it back in her face. He'd seen

the hurt in her eyes when he'd hurled his accusations at her, and he'd ignored it. Too consumed by his own torment to think clearly.

Alex's heart thumped. The knowledge that he'd made the most horrendous mistake tore at his gut. A dreadful feeling of panic spread through him and a tight knot formed in his chest.

He had to undo the damage he'd done.

He swung back and rang the doorbell. When there was no answer he knelt down and pushed open the letter box.

'Phoebe?'

'Go away!'

He guessed he deserved that but she wasn't getting rid of him that easily. 'I want to talk to you.'

'There's nothing left to say.'

He hammered on the door. 'Open the door.'

'No.'

'Please. I'm on my knees. I feel like an idiot.'

'Good.'

'I'll sit on the doorbell if I have to.'

Silence. Then the door flung open and the relief that he'd been waiting for earlier finally came.

'Fine. What?'

Phoebe's face was white and drawn, her eyes were huge and glassy and his heart wrenched at the realisation that it was all because of him.

'I'm sorry I accused you of going to the press. I know you'd never have done that.'

'So why did you?'

'Instinct. Habit. You're right. I *have* let mistrust influence my decisions over the years. But apparently not any more.'

'Apparently?'

The lack of emotion in her voice rocked his confidence and sent a chill running down his spine. 'I think I do trust you. And it *is* personal. You're the only person I've ever not worried about letting me down.'

A faint light flickered in her eyes. 'And?'

Alex frowned. 'And what?' If he was being honest, he'd been expecting her to fall into his arms, draw him back inside and let him prove to her how sorry he was for being such an idiot. 'Doesn't it make any difference?'

'To what?'

Fear clawed at his stomach and a sense of panic began to spread through him. 'Well, to us. Our affair.'

'Not really.' She sighed deeply. 'Alex. Look. Please go. I don't want this and I don't want to see you any more. So please. Just go.'

The door clicked shut and Alex reeled. For a moment he just stared at it in shock. Then a searing pain began to burn in his chest as he realised that whatever had existed between them, whatever it might have turned into, he'd destroyed it.

CHAPTER FIFTEEN

PHOEBE SPENT THE rest of the weekend wandering around listlessly, her head filled with thoughts of Alex. Every second of every minute, day and night. Where he was, what he might be doing, who he might be seeing.

So much for thinking she didn't want him. Didn't need him. She felt as if she'd suddenly lost a vital organ. She shouldn't have shut the door on him. She should have taken what she thought he might have been offering: the chance to resume their relationship and get back to the hot sex.

So why hadn't she? Why had no-strings-attached sex suddenly seemed so meaningless? When had it become not enough?

Over the course of the weekend Phoebe drove herself slowly mental with self-analysis and self recrimination. Tormenting herself with those annoying 'what if's and 'if only's.

By Sunday evening she was in such a state that she had no idea why or how she ended up standing on the doorstep of her parents' house. All she knew was that she was climbing the walls of her own place and she had nowhere else to go.

Her mother opened the door, her father standing just behind her, and for a second they both stared at her in surprise. 'Phoebe?' said her mother, recovering first and peering at her closely. 'Are you all right?'

'Fine,' Phoebe said, then promptly burst into tears.

Unable to stop the torrent that streamed down her cheeks and the racking sobs that shook her body, Phoebe let herself be pulled into the house and ushered into the kitchen. In the midst of her misery, she felt her mother gently push her down into a chair and wait while she bawled her eyes out.

'Sorry about that,' she said with a watery smile once she'd cried herself out and could actually find her voice. 'Where did Dad go?'

'His study. Tears aren't really his thing.'

'Nor yours.' She pulled a string of tissues out of the box her mother had thrust in front of her.

Her mother frowned. 'Well, no. But I've never seen you cry. Not even when you fell out of that tree. I was worried.'

Worried? Phoebe hiccupped and blew her nose. Her eyes stung and her throat was raw. 'I don't really know why I'm here,' she said hoarsely.

Her mother sat down on the opposite side of the kitchen table. 'Phoebe, I know I'm not the most…demonstrative…of mothers, but if you tell me what's wrong, I might be able to help.'

'I don't know what's wrong.'

'Is it work?'

'No. Work's fine.'

'Is it a man?'

'Yes. No.' She wailed in frustration and dropped her head on the kitchen table. 'I don't know.'

'The man in the magazine?'

Her head shot up. 'Don't tell me you saw that as well?'

'Your sister told me I might like to see a copy. Especially since I'd introduced you to him at our party.'

Phoebe groaned and buried her face in her hands. 'I met him before that. I work with his sister.'

'Is she in venture capital too?'

She glanced up and couldn't help smiling at the hope in her mother's voice. 'I'm afraid she designs handbags.'

'Oh well, never mind. Is any of the article true?'

'Some. Mum, what do I do? I can't eat. I can't sleep. I'm a wreck and I'm worried it's going to affect my work.'

'I can't pretend to understand PR, and you know it's not what we'd have chosen for you, but we brought you up to have belief in yourself. That whatever course of action you take, you have the confidence that it's the right one because you've given it thought. Weighed up the pros and cons.'

How could she weigh up any pros or cons when she didn't have a clue about anything?

'I'm very proud of everything you've achieved, you know.'

'Really?' she sniffed.

Her mother nodded thoughtfully. 'I don't worry about you nearly as much as I worry about the other two.'

'Why?'

'I always knew you'd be all right. Your siblings, on the other hand, are harder.'

Bewilderment muddled her brain. 'I always thought you admired their ruthlessness. The way they don't let emotion dictate to them.'

Her mother shook her head gently. 'Emotion isn't a bad thing.'

Wasn't it? 'It scares me. Alex scares me. He distorts my judgement and wipes away my self-control.'

'That's not his fault. He seems like a nice man.'

Huh. 'Nice isn't the word. He's manipulative and arrogant and annoying and...' Gorgeous, protective, passionate.

'Yet you love him anyway.'

Phoebe froze. 'No, I don't.'

Her mother shot her a shrewd look and Phoebe blinked. She couldn't be in love with Alex. Could she? Her mind raced. 'Oh, God. I think I do.'

'You think?'

'I don't know. I mean... I've never been in love before. How do I know if that's what this...thing... is?'

'How does he make you feel?'

'Like I could rule the world.'

'So what are you doing here?'

'I told him I never wanted to see him again.'

'Oh dear,' said her mother. 'I can't imagine that would have gone down very well.'

'It was his fault. He accused me of using our relationship to further my business.'

'Oh.' Her mother frowned.

'Quite.'

'Then you need to talk. Communication is the thing. Give him the chance to explain. To apologise.'

'I did and he did.'

'And you still turned him away? I'm lost.'

'So am I,' Phoebe wailed. 'Totally and utterly lost. I hate that my mental stability depends on him. I hate that he can do this to me.'

'Phoebe, darling, have faith in yourself. Loving someone and marrying them doesn't mean you have to give up your independence. And so what if it does?

At times, you'll have to rely on him. At others he'll rely on you.'

Phoebe hiccupped. What would it be like to have someone to lean on from time to time? Someone strong and dependable. Someone to protect you when you were attacked, to pick you up when you fell. Someone like Alex. Her heart began to thud.

'If he's The One, it doesn't make you vulnerable and it doesn't mean you're any weaker.'

Phoebe gave a shaky laugh. 'I can't believe you're talking about "The One".'

'What do you think your father is?'

Her jaw dropped.

'Don't look so surprised. I wouldn't have given up my own independence for anyone else. Is Alex The One?'

'I think he might be.' Her heart leapt and then plummeted. 'But I'm not sure I am.'

Her mother tilted her head. 'Did you ever look at the pictures in that magazine?'

'Of course.'

'Properly?'

'Not that closely.'

Her mother got up and rummaged around in the stack of papers on the counter. 'Look again,' she said, opening the magazine and putting it in front of Phoebe.

Phoebe ignored the grainy photo that had been taken while she and Alex had been kissing beneath the pergola and concentrated on the picture in the restaurant.

An empty bottle of wine sat on the red and white checked tablecloth. They'd been talking and laughing and desperately trying to keep their hands off each other. The way they hadn't been able to hold back any longer and had rushed back to his house for a night of passion made her breathless just thinking about it. The dreamy expression on her face… The light in her eye… It was obvious to anyone with half a brain cell that she was nuts about him. Up until now, she'd clearly been lacking even that half a brain cell.

'What am I looking for?'

'Just look.'

She huffed and switched to the picture of the two of them strolling in the park. Alex's arm was around her shoulders, pulling her into him and she was smiling up at him.

She leaned closer. Oh, goodness. Phoebe's heart began to thump crazily. The expression on his face…the look in his eyes… Exactly the same as hers had been in the restaurant.

'He adores you.'

Phoebe went very cold. The image of his face, white and stunned, when she'd told him to go away for good flashed into her head. Maybe he'd have told her if she'd let him. But she hadn't given him the chance. She'd just pushed him away.

She began to shake uncontrollably. What had she done? *What had she done?*

'You'd better go and find him.'

Finding Alex was easier said than done. He seemed to have disappeared off the face of the earth.

Phoebe staked out his house but he didn't show up. His secretary must have known where he'd gone, but if she did she was keeping the information to herself, despite Phoebe's best attempts at trying to wheedle it out of her. And Jo was as much in the dark as she was.

It was driving Phoebe demented.

Now she'd acknowledged that she was in fact in love with Alex all she wanted to do was tell him. Get down on her knees and grovel. Persuade him to admit he loved her too and see if they couldn't make something of whatever they'd had before.

Simple. Or it would be if she only knew where he was.

Maybe she could hire an investigator. Whoever Alex had used to check her out had produced incredible results in a breathtakingly short period of time. She could do the same.

Or perhaps she'd resort to desperate measures and contact each and every one of the people who'd attended his party on the island. Someone was bound to know where he was.

What the hell. She was desperate. This was no time for dignity. She'd beg if she had to. She opened the relevant file on her computer and then went very still.

A flashbulb went off in her head. Her heart pounded and she felt more alive than she had in days. That was where Alex was.

He'd escaped. To the Ilha das Palmeiras.

CHAPTER SIXTEEN

PHOEBE WATCHED JIM'S boat as it grew smaller and smaller and felt sicker now than at any point in her journey to Alex's island. And that was despite the turbulent flight and the even choppier boat ride.

Her stomach was churning and adrenalin pounded through her veins. With her nerves rocketing, Phoebe turned and stared up at the house. Her heart thumped. Alex was in there. Her future happiness was in there. Hopefully.

But what sort of mood would she find him in? Would he be pleased to see her? Or horrified? Would he even be prepared to listen to her when she'd so recklessly pushed him away?

Doubts began to assail her from all sides. Maybe she should have called Maggie and established that Alex was in fact on the island. Maybe she should have waited until he got back to London, as he surely would have had to have done at some point.

Oh God. She hadn't weighed up the pros and cons of this course of action at all. She'd never acted so rashly. But then she'd never needed to.

Phoebe swallowed back the nerves and told herself that a faint heart had never achieved anything.

The spatter of great fat raindrops galvanised her into action. She hauled her bag onto her shoulder and raced up the steps to the house. She reached the front door just as the heavens opened.

Her heart thundered with anticipation and exertion. She was so close. Just a few more minutes and she'd know her fate one way or another.

She turned the handle and pulled, but nothing happened. She tried again, rattling it back and forth, but it was locked. Panic swept through her. She bashed on the door with her fist and shouted Alex's name. But there was no answer and no sound of footsteps striding towards the door.

Alex wasn't there. So where was he? *Where was he?* Could she have got it wrong? Was he in fact back in London? In the arms of another woman, one who wouldn't blow hot and cold and push him away. Her heart clenched. No, she wouldn't believe that. Alex wouldn't do that. Not if he loved her.

But supposing she'd read too much into that photo? Fancied she'd seen something that didn't exist simply because that was what she wanted to see? Or what if he *had* felt something for her but as she'd rejected him had decided that that was that and had moved on?

Wind lashed at the palm trees. The rain turned torrential and plastered her clothes to her body. Phoebe shivered and rubbed her arms. Her knees shook. Her heart twisted. No. She wouldn't let that happen. If that was the case, she'd just have to do everything in her power to get him to love her again. She was *not* going to fail.

She cupped her hands to the glass to see if there were any signs he'd been there. But she could see nothing except the blurred outline of the Jeep on the other side of the house.

Phoebe's heart leapt with encouragement. Alex *was* here. Somewhere. And it was up to her to find him.

Thunder crackled above her and lightning sliced through the sky. She dropped her bag and raced across the terrace. She tore along the paths, searching desperately, hoping wildly, not caring that rain sluiced over her, drenching her clothes, her skin, her hair. She stumbled to the top of the steps that led down to the sea and frantically scoured the beach. She looked for him until her body ached inside and out. But with every passing minute, hope faded.

Because there was no sign of him.

Wherever he was, Alex didn't want to be found.

As the realisation dawned Phoebe's energy drained and her heart broke. Utterly defeated and exhausted, she felt a flood of emotion crash over her. Despair, misery, hopelessness all piled in on top of each other and she knew she'd never felt pain like it. Tears mingled with the rain and she dashed them away with the backs of her hands.

She'd been so sure she'd find him. So sure she'd be able to fix the mess she'd made of things. And the knowledge that she'd failed was agonising.

The dark stormy grey of the huge waves rolling towards the shore reminded her of Alex's eyes the last time she'd seen him, and as memories cascaded into her head she felt yet more misery well up inside her.

Oh, God, would it ever end?

She felt as weak and vulnerable as a little boat being battered by the waves, completely at the mercy of something far too powerful to comprehend.

And then her heart skipped a beat.

Hang on.

She snapped her gaze to the jetty.

Alex's yacht was gone.

She'd been in such a state when she'd got off Jim's boat that she hadn't noticed, but it wasn't there.

Hope flared in her chest. And then her heart began to pound. He must be out there. Somewhere in the vastness of the ocean. In the middle of this raging storm.

Fear clutched at her breast and obliterated the relief. What if something happened to him? He was out there because of her. She started to shake as pure terror began to flood through her. She hadn't even told him she loved him.

Phoebe tore down the steps and charged onto the jetty. She scanned the sea, but the visibility was getting worse and she could see nothing but great mountains of water.

Her mind began to race. Her imagination went into overdrive. Scenario after scenario ripped through her head and she filled with the agonising awareness that she could well have lost him.

As wretchedness scythed through her and a wave washed over her Phoebe's legs gave way and she crumpled into a heap.

Even the weather had turned against him, thought Alex grimly, dredging up every ounce of strength he possessed to keep the yacht upright.

He'd been out in worse, but not much. He braced himself for yet another wave that bore down on him. A whoosh of water crashed over the stern and as the boat groaned and creaked Alex staggered beneath the force of it. His muscles stung with the effort of holding the tiller steady. Every bone in his body was battered and bruised and he could feel a cut on his cheek.

He should have checked the forecast. He should have turned back at the first hint of rain. He should have been watching the wave patterns and paying attention to the darkening of the skies. He should have remembered that storms in this part of the world tended to set in in a matter of minutes.

But then there were lots of things he should have done over the past week.

He should have realised the depths of his feelings for Phoebe sooner, and he should have stayed in London and insisted on hammering things out with her instead of running off to lick his wounds here.

Because what good had that done him? None at all. All he'd done here was sit and brood and ache for her. At least, he thought as adrenalin coursed through his veins, it proved he could still feel something.

If he ever got back to the island alive, and right now the chances of that happening were looking pretty slim, he'd head straight back to London. He'd wine and dine Phoebe and woo her properly until her resistance buckled under the relentless pressure. Once he'd got her back into his bed and rendered her all soft and warm and amenable, he'd set about making her love him as much as he'd realised he loved her. However long it took. He didn't care. He was fully prepared to devote the rest of his life to the endeavour.

And as that was the case, he thought determinedly, he would not be consigning himself to a watery grave any time soon. His heart pumping wildly with renewed energy, Alex hoisted the storm sail, set the stern to the waves and concentrated on steering the yacht to safety before the storm bashed them both to bits.

How long she'd been sitting there when something slammed into the side of the jetty, Phoebe had no idea. She was numb with cold and despair. The thought that she might never see Alex, might never hold him again, had been tearing away at her and her whole body ached unbearably with grief. She trembled and wrapped her arms around herself and waited for the icy wave to wash over her. For all she cared, it could knock her into the sea, drag her under and carry her away.

When it didn't, and she heard the slap of wet ropes landing on wood inches from her knees, her heart began to hammer and her eyes flew open.

For a moment Phoebe just stared. Then she rubbed her eyes and blinked and felt everything inside her spring to life. Because there, right in front of her, was the *Phoenix Three*. A bit battered but in one piece and she didn't think she'd ever been so happy to see forty feet of gleaming white fibreglass.

Relief thundered through her. She hadn't lost him. At least not to the storm. He was there. Alive. Unclipping himself from the guardrail and stepping off the boat.

'Alex,' she croaked, lurching to her feet and beginning to shiver uncontrollably.

But he was throwing loops of rope over the bollards and clearly hadn't heard her so she swallowed and tried again. 'Alex!'

Alex froze and spun round. 'Phoebe?' For a moment he just stood there and stared at her. Then she caught a flash of raw unguarded emotion on his face and her legs automatically propelled her towards him.

She stopped a foot away, suddenly completely at a loss as to what to say. The speech she'd spent the entire flight over carefully practising flew out of her head. Because, the way he was glowering at her, he didn't look as if he was pleased to see her at all.

'What the hell are you doing here?' he said roughly, wiping the water from his eyes and looking her up and down as if he couldn't quite believe she was there. 'How long have you been out here?'

'I don't know,' she croaked and wrapped her arms around herself.

Alex frowned, then shrugged off his oilskin and helped her into it. And then as the warmth from his body enveloped her Phoebe couldn't hold back. She launched herself at him, flinging her arms around his neck, pulling his head down and pressing her mouth to his, pouring everything she'd gone through into a kiss that shook her to the soles of her feet.

'I'm sorry,' she mumbled over and over again against his lips, wanting to never let him go.

Alex's arms whipped around her waist and crushed her tighter against him. He kissed her back as if his life depended on it. She moaned and sank into him and his hands came up to cup her face. He cradled her as if she was the most precious thing he'd ever held and Phoebe nearly collapsed with relief. He *was* pleased to see her.

But as heat spread through her all the feelings she'd been protected from by the numbness came crashing down on her and she suddenly found she was shaking. Sobs began to rack her body.

'Phoebe?' Alex lifted his head and gazed down at her, his eyes blazing with heat and desire and concern.

'I thought you were dead!' she yelled, pulling back and thumping him in the chest.

He caught her shoulders and pulled her closer to stop her thumps and her shivering. 'Why would I be dead?' he said soothingly.

'I thought you'd capsized and drowned and been eaten by sharks.'

Alex held her tighter. 'There aren't any sharks round here.'

'Or kidnapped by pirates.'

'Not many pirates either.'

She could feel him smile against her hair, and she jerked back and glared up at him, her eyes swimming with tears. 'Don't joke. What did you think you were doing going out in a flimsy boat like that in weather like this?'

'I've been through worse.'

'But I haven't,' she cried, beginning to pummel him again. 'I thought I'd lost you. I thought I'd lost you and I'd never be able to tell you how sorry I am. And I am sorry, really sorry.'

Alex caught her wrists. 'So am I.'

'You don't need to be,' she said wretchedly. 'I'm the one who told you to go away.'

'Phoebe, I—' he broke off suddenly and her heart lurched crazily at the look in his eye '—am not having this conversation in the pouring rain,' he muttered, sweeping her into his arms, oilskin and all, and carrying her down the jetty and along the beach.

'Where are we going?' she said, not really caring as long as she could stay in his arms for ever. She wanted to burrow beneath his soaking clothes and warm herself against his skin.

'The beach hut.'

'I didn't know there was one,' she mumbled against his chest.

'It's very basic.'

He backed into the wooden hut nestling among the trees at the edge of the beach and then set her on her feet. He was right, she thought, glancing around. It was very basic. Just one room. With a bed. Unmade and clearly slept in. But as long as it contained Alex, it felt like home to her.

In the blissful warmth of the hut, she felt the terror and anguish melt away. Then she caught the look in his eyes and nerves swooped in to take over. 'Have you been staying here?' she said, keeping her eyes fixed to the floor.

'Yes.'

'Why?'

'Too many memories everywhere else.'

'Of what?'

'Of you.'

Her head shot up. Alex was leaning against the wall of the hut, his arms folded over his chest, and watching her.

'Good memories?' she asked nervously.

'Disturbing memories.'

'Me too,' she said, her heart thundering. She'd come this far. She had to see it through to the end. Whatever the outcome. 'I've missed you,' she said, her voice cracking. 'I know I drove you away, but, I swear, give me another chance and—' she scoured his face for the tiniest flicker of encouragement but his expression was inscrutable and her courage suddenly deserted her '—perhaps we could resume our affair.'

Alex tilted his head and stared at her for what seemed like hours. 'No,' he said eventually.

'No?' Phoebe suddenly felt very cold. Oh, God. Maybe she *had* got it all wrong. Maybe it was way too late.

'I don't want an affair.'

Phoebe thought she might break apart. 'Alex, please—' She didn't care that she was begging.

He pushed himself off the wall and walked slowly towards her. 'It's a good thing you're here.'

No, it wasn't. It was heartbreaking. She should never have come. She took a step back and swallowed down the aching lump in her throat. 'Is it?'

Alex nodded. 'Saves me a bumpy ride back to London,' he said, a faint smile appearing on his lips.

Phoebe jerked to a halt and her heart began to bang around so wildly she feared it might leap out of her chest. 'You were going to come back?' Was it too much to hope that he'd been planning to return for her? 'Why?' she said shakily.

'I came here to escape. It hasn't worked.'

He stopped in front of her and Phoebe began to tremble. 'Escape from what?'

'The way I feel about you.'

'How do you feel about me?' she breathed, and time seemed to stand still as if aware of how much hung on his answer.

He searched her features and brushed a clump of hair from her face. 'I love you. So I don't just want an affair. I want everything.'

For a moment Phoebe went dizzy and then her chest filled with such happiness that she didn't think she'd be able to contain it. Without warning tears sprang up from nowhere and began to spill down her cheeks.

'Why are you crying?' he murmured, gently wiping them away with his thumbs. 'Is the fact that I love you really that appalling?'

'It's not appalling at all.' She sniffed, giving him a watery smile. 'It's the loveliest thing I've ever heard.'

'That's better.'

'You really love me?'

'I do.'

'Even like this?' She pointed to her red-nosed, puffy-eyed, bedraggled self.

Alex laughed softly. 'Any way you come. I should have told you I loved you the last time I saw you.' The laughter faded from his eyes. 'I just want you, Phoebe. All of you. For ever.'

Phoebe closed the gap between them and ran her hands up his chest to hold his face. 'You have me. Everything I have, everything I am, it's yours. I love you too. So much. When I think about you... Out there...'

She shook and Alex wrapped her in his arms. 'Don't think,' he said, capturing her mouth in a sizzling kiss filled with love and promise. His heart beat in time with hers, and as she felt a smile spread throughout her body Phoebe wondered what she'd done to deserve this much happiness.

'You're still thinking,' he said, lifting his head a fraction and arching an eyebrow.

'I am. Want to know what about?' she murmured as the familiar beat of desire began to unfurl inside her.

'What?'

Phoebe wound her arms around his neck and smiled up at him. 'I'm thinking we should get out of these wet things.'

Coming Next Month

in **Harlequin Presents®**. Available September 28, 2010.

#2945 PUBLIC MARRIAGE, PRIVATE SECRETS
Helen Bianchin

#2946 EMILY AND THE NOTORIOUS PRINCE
India Grey
The Balfour Brides

#2947 INNOCENT SECRETARY...ACCIDENTALLY PREGNANT
Carol Marinelli

#2948 BRIDE IN A GILDED CAGE
Abby Green
Bride on Approval

#2949 HIS VIRGIN ACQUISITION
Maisey Yates

#2950 MAJESTY, MISTRESS...MISSING HEIR
Caitlin Crews

Coming Next Month

in **Harlequin Presents®** EXTRA. Available October 12, 2010.

#121 POWERFUL GREEK, HOUSEKEEPER WIFE
Robyn Donald
The Greek Tycoons

#122 THE GOOD GREEK WIFE?
Kate Walker
The Greek Tycoons

#123 BOARDROOM RIVALS, BEDROOM FIREWORKS!
Kimberly Lang
Back in His Bed

#124 UNFINISHED BUSINESS WITH THE DUKE
Heidi Rice
Back in His Bed

LARGER-PRINT BOOKS!

PASSION GUARANTEED SEDUCTION

GET 2 FREE LARGER-PRINT
NOVELS PLUS 2 FREE GIFTS!

YES! Please send me 2 FREE LARGER-PRINT Harlequin Presents® novels and my 2 FREE gifts (gifts are worth about $10). After receiving them, if I don't wish to receive any more books, I can return the shipping statement marked "cancel." If I don't cancel, I will receive 6 brand-new novels every month and be billed just $4.55 per book in the U.S. or $5.24 per book in Canada. That's a saving of at least 13% off the cover price! It's quite a bargain! Shipping and handling is just 50¢ per book.* I understand that accepting the 2 free books and gifts places me under no obligation to buy anything. I can always return a shipment and cancel at any time. Even if I never buy another book, the two free books and gifts are mine to keep forever.

176/376 HDN E5NG

Name _____ (PLEASE PRINT) _____

Address _____ Apt. # _____

City _____ State/Prov. _____ Zip/Postal Code _____

Signature (if under 18, a parent or guardian must sign) _____

Mail to the **Harlequin Reader Service:**
IN U.S.A.: P.O. Box 1867, Buffalo, NY 14240-1867
IN CANADA: P.O. Box 609, Fort Erie, Ontario L2A 5X3

Not valid for current subscribers to Harlequin Presents Larger-Print books.

Are you a subscriber to Harlequin Presents books
and want to receive the larger-print edition?
Call 1-800-873-8635 today!

* Terms and prices subject to change without notice. Prices do not include applicable taxes. Sales tax applicable in N.Y. Canadian residents will be charged applicable provincial taxes and GST. Offer not valid in Quebec. This offer is limited to one order per household. All orders subject to approval. Credit or debit balances in a customer's account(s) may be offset by any other outstanding balance owed by or to the customer. Please allow 4 to 6 weeks for delivery. Offer available while quantities last.

Your Privacy: Harlequin Books is committed to protecting your privacy. Our Privacy Policy is available online at www.eHarlequin.com or upon request from the Reader Service. From time to time we make our lists of customers available to reputable third parties who may have a product or service of interest to you. If you would prefer we not share your name and address, please check here. ☐

Help us get it right—We strive for accurate, respectful and relevant communications. To clarify or modify your communication preferences, visit us at www.ReaderService.com/consumerschoice.

HPLP10R

HARLEQUIN®

A Romance

FOR EVERY MOOD™

Spotlight on

Inspirational

Wholesome romances
that touch the heart and soul.

See the next page
to enjoy a sneak peek from
the Love Inspired® inspirational series.

CATINSPLI10

*See below for a sneak peek at
our inspirational line, Love Inspired®.
Introducing HIS HOLIDAY BRIDE
by bestselling author Jillian Hart*

Autumn Granger gave her horse rein to slide toward the town's new sheriff.

"Hey, there." The man in a brand-new Stetson, black T-shirt, jeans and riding boots held up a hand in greeting. He stepped away from his four-wheel drive with "Sheriff" in black on the doors and waded through the grasses. "I'm new around here."

"I'm Autumn Granger."

"Nice to meet you, Miss Granger. I'm Ford Sherman, from Chicago." He knuckled back his hat, revealing the most handsome face she'd ever seen. Big blue eyes contrasted with his sun-tanned complexion.

"I'm guessing you haven't seen much open land. Out here, you've got to keep an eye on cows or they're going to tear your vehicle apart."

"What?" He whipped around. Sure enough, mammoth black-and-white creatures had started to gnaw on his four-wheel drive. They clustered like a mob, mouths and tongues and teeth bent on destruction. One cow tried to pry the wiper off the windshield, another chewed on the side mirror. Several leaned through the open window, licking the seats.

"Move along, little dogie." He didn't know the first thing about cattle.

The entire herd swiveled their heads to study him curiously. Not a single hoof shifted. The animals soon returned to chewing, licking, digging through his possessions.

Autumn laughed, a warm and wonderful sound. "Thanks,

I needed that." She then pulled a bag from behind her saddle and waved it at the cows. "Look what I have, guys. Cookies."

Cows swung in her direction, and dozens of liquid brown eyes brightened with cookie hopes. As she circled the car, the cattle bounded after her. The earth shook with the force of their powerful hooves.

"Next time, you're on your own, city boy." She tipped her hat. The cowgirl stayed on his mind, the sweetest thing he had ever seen.

*Will Ford be able to stick it out in the country
to find out more about Autumn?
Find out in HIS HOLIDAY BRIDE
by bestselling author Jillian Hart,
available in October 2010
only from Love Inspired®.*

Copyright © 2010 by Jill Strickler

SHLIEXP1010

FROM #1 *NEW YORK TIMES*
AND *USA TODAY* BESTSELLING AUTHOR

DEBBIE MACOMBER

Mrs. Miracle on 34th Street...

This Christmas, Emily Merkle (just call her Mrs. Miracle)
is working in the toy department at Finley's, the last
family-owned department store in Manhattan.

Her boss (who happens to be the owner's son) has placed
an order for a large number of high-priced robots, which
he hopes will give the business a much-needed boost. In
fact, Jake Finley's counting on it.

Holly Larson is counting on that robot, too. She's been
looking after her eight-year-old nephew, Gabe, ever since
her widowed brother was deployed overseas. Holly plans
to buy Gabe a robot—which she can't afford—because
she's determined to make Christmas special.

But this Christmas will be different—thanks to Mrs.
Miracle. Next to bringing children joy, her favorite activity
is giving romance a nudge. Fortunately, Jake and Holly
are receptive to her "hints." And thanks to Mrs. Miracle,
Christmas takes on new meaning for Jake. For all of them!

Call Me Mrs. Miracle

Available wherever books are sold
September 28!

MIRA®

www.MIRABooks.com

MDM2819